# MISSION
## LIBERTAD

### By Lizette M. Lantigua

Pauline
BOOKS & MEDIA
Boston

Library of Congress Cataloging-in-Publication Data

Lantigua, Lizette M.
  Mission libertad / by Lizette M. Lantigua.
      p. cm.
  Summary: With his parents, fourteen-year-old Luis escapes from Communist Cuba in 1979 and goes to live in Maryland with relatives who teach him about American life and God, but Luis, eager to fulfill a promise to his Abuela, manages to do so under the eyes of spies.
  ISBN 978-0-8198-4900-7
  [1. Immigrants--Fiction. 2. Cubans--United States--Fiction. 3. Family life--Maryland--Fiction. 4. Spies--Fiction. 5. Refugees--Fiction. 6. Emigration and immigration--Fiction. 7. Maryland--History--20th century--Fiction. 8. Cuba--History--1959-1990--Fiction.] I. Title.
  PZ7.L2924Mis 2012
  [Fic]--dc23

                          2012009983

Design by Mary Joseph Peterson, FSP

Cover art by Penny Hauffe

Published by Pauline Books & Media, 50 Saint Pauls Avenue, Boston, MA 02130-3491

Printed in U.S.A.

ML VSAUSAPEOILL4-24J12-03561 4900-6

www.pauline.org

Pauline Books & Media is the publishing house of the Daughters of St. Paul, an international congregation of women religious serving the Church with the communications media.

1 2 3 4 5 6 7 8 9                                        16 15 14 13 12

*Thanking God for all his many blessings,
and my family for all their support—especially
my Little Flower for reading the book first!*

# 1 UNO

The smell of wet grass filled the dark night. Four-teen-year-old Luisito picked his way along the path by the light of the full moon, the only sound the squelching of mud beneath his feet. It was June 10, 1979, and he was on the run.

His heart beat so fast he felt sure the sound would alert the police. He could barely see his father's silhouette in front of him. He grasped his mother's hand firmly and led her along the path. Luisito swatted at mosquitoes and other bugs that smacked his face as he ran. At the end of the path a man, whom Luisito could hardly make out in the dark, pointed to the ground. There, hidden in the bushes, lay a homemade raft. Wordlessly, the man helped

Luisito and his dad drag the raft into the quiet waters. He then patted Luisito's dad on the back. "*Buena suerte*," he whispered, disappearing back along the path. *Good luck*, Luisito thought. *Yes, we will need it.*

Luisito and his parents climbed aboard the raft. It was a flimsy little contraption. Would it actually take them the ninety miles across the ocean to the United States?

Luisito felt a knot of fear in the middle of his stomach and an urgent need to go to the bathroom, but there was no time. Elena, Luisito's mother, wore a look of quiet determination. Her dark brown eyes shone in the night, her face pale with anxiety. Now it was she who grasped Luisito's hand. He noticed that her palms were sweaty.

He could only imagine how he looked. The left sleeve of his cotton t-shirt had been torn on a branch as he ran along the muddy path, and every time he touched his dirty blond hair gnats would pop out.

Miguel, Luisito's father, pointed to the oars. They didn't want to use the noisy motor just yet. Luisito, imitating his father, used his oar to push the raft out of the shallow area and into the deep ocean. Luisito remembered his father mentioning in the past how rafts were hard for the radar in Cuban patrol boats to detect. This brought him a sense of relief as they slowly rowed away from shore. At first, their rowing was awkward, but soon Luisito and Miguel developed a comfortable rhythm. They rowed farther and farther away from shore and into the vast dark ocean.

"Let's take a break," Miguel said, whispering even though no one was around for miles. They drifted aimlessly as they stretched their arms. The ocean was still calm, and Luisito's heart started to beat normally again. His stomach began to relax. He tried to make sense of what had just happened.

A few hours ago, his whole life had changed. He had been sleeping on the sofa bed in the living room. It had seemed like just another hot summer night in Havana. Luisito had spent all day waiting in line with his grandmother to buy bread and rice. By evening he was exhausted. He expected that in a few weeks he would be sent to work in the sugar cane fields. Every summer Cuban children twelve years and older were required to leave their homes and were sent to the country to cut sugar cane and teach poor children to read. The idea had seemed noble at first, and he and his friends had been excited. But after a grueling month at the camp cutting cane under a melting sun, with hardly any food to eat and a combination of dirty mattresses and filthy bathrooms, the novelty had begun to fade. Luisito had come to dread the idea of going back.

Tonight, he had gone to sleep early. It felt hot and stuffy on the sofa bed. He tossed and turned. The mattress made an irritating squeaky sound. He was afraid he would disturb his grandmother. They shared the living room, while his parents had the only bedroom of their tiny apartment. He remembered finally mustering the energy to get up to open the living room window. He felt his way in the dark. There had been another power outage in the neighborhood, and it would probably last until dawn. The cracked marble floor felt cool under his bare feet as he walked past the bookcases and right by his grandma, or *abuela* (ah-BWAY-la), who was sleeping on her *pin pan pun*, a simple cot. Luisito loved to say the words. They sounded more like a noise than a noun.

"Go back to bed, Luisito," Abuela whispered, startling him.

"It's hot, Abuela," Luisito protested.

"Don't touch the windows. Not tonight, Luisito," Abuela said. In a country where fear ruled, Luisito had learned from an early age not to ask many questions. If his grandmother thought it was best to have the windows just slightly opened, then there was probably a good reason. He tumbled back into his bed, wondering. He could hear Abuela mumbling her prayers in the quiet night. He also heard her sniffle. Maybe it was her allergies again.

Luisito had closed his eyes, and before he knew it he had fallen sound asleep.

"Luisito!" his mother whispered. She shook him awake.

"Luisito, wake up," Abuela said as well. Luisito opened his eyes. The room was still dark but Abuela held a small lit candle. It was very warm in the room. Abuela looked at him with teary eyes. His parents told him to dress rapidly and to stay quiet.

"What's happening? Is it a raid?" Luisito whispered. It was not uncommon for the police to search people's homes or even to take citizens away in the middle of the night to question them.

"Hurry! Get up. We need to leave," his mother said.

Luisito's heart pounded quickly as he slipped on a pair of shorts and a t-shirt over his pajama shorts.

"*¡Vamos!* Come!" Miguel said, grabbing his son by the elbow.

Luisito turned to follow his father and was met by Abuela, reaching out to hug him. Her brown eyes were squinting and her cheeks felt wet as she embraced him. Everything was happening too fast. This felt more like a nightmare than reality.

"*Que Dios te acompañe,* Luisito," she whispered, her lips trembling as she tried to hold back her tears. She pulled him closer and whispered something urgently in his ear. Confused, Luisito strained to hear. "Don't forget, Luisito!" she said, pulling away and wiping her eyes. "I trust you. It's important."

He nodded to Abuela in agreement. He would try not to forget. He repeated the information one more time in his head.

"*¡Apúrate!* Hurry! Hurry!" Elena said, her eyes red and swollen from crying. At that moment, Luisito realized what they were about to do, and he was scared.

They opened their apartment door carefully, and quietly walked down the steps of the old Havana mansion, which had belonged to his family before the government took it and converted into a four-unit apartment building. Luisito and his family now lived confined to the upstairs one-bedroom unit. Luisito was careful not to make a sound as they passed the apartment of their next-door neighbor, Ofelia, who belonged to the *comité de barrio*. If she heard, she would certainly snitch on them.

The *comité* was the neighborhood watch committee whose members kept a close eye on activities of everyone on the block and reported them to the government. If the Ramirezes were discovered, they would be imprisoned— or worse.

As they walked around the corner they looked up at Ofelia's window. Her apartment was dark. They were safe, for now.

When they reached the main road, Miguel signaled that they should cross the street. They walked quickly behind some buildings. At the next block, a man was waiting in an old truck. He motioned to them to get in. If they had taken their own car, the noise would have awakened the neighbors. Miguel opened the truck's passenger door and the Ramirez family scrambled in. They were quiet all through the thirty-minute ride to the beach. That's when Luisito felt his heart pounding in his chest and sweat trickling down his back. The man didn't say a word, and neither did Luisito's parents, until they came to a stop. The driver parked near some bushes, then led the way on foot through the tall grass toward the sand. There they found a homemade raft.

Luisito thought of all this as he floated with his parents in the ten-foot raft, now a mere speck in the vast ocean. The raft was made of three large Soviet inner tubes, tied together and wrapped in fabric, with wooden planks across the top. The family also had a white cotton sheet to use as a makeshift sail. Wooden oars were well secured on both sides of the raft, and some provisions were securely tied to the sides. A small motor was attached to the raft.

Luisito felt the warm salty breeze as he sat in the raft. Occasionally, Miguel used the oars to guide the raft in the right direction. The waves were gentle. The current was a good accomplice, helping them along their course. As the raft made its way through the dark waters, Luisito thought, *My desk at school will be empty tomorrow. Teachers at the preschool will be wondering why my mother has not shown up for work, and nurses will be looking all over the hospital for my father, Dr. Miguel Ramirez. No one will guess we are escaping to freedom.*

Either from stress or from fear, the Ramirez family remained silent even now, when no one could possibly hear them. Everything around them looked dark. Luisito wondered how his father had been able to purchase the raft, who had helped him, and how long he had been planning all this. He wanted to ask but didn't know where to begin. All Luisito knew for sure was that his family was headed in a direction where life would be different.

# 2 DOS

As Luisito sat holding on to a couple of oars, thoughts of Abuela, his friends, and his neighborhood bombarded his mind, but he pushed them aside. Survival was the only thing that mattered now.

"Papi, how long till we hit shore?" Luisito asked, finally breaking the silence.

"About two days if everything goes well with this small motor I am about to start," Miguel said as he ran his fingers through his uncombed light-brown hair. His wide blue eyes, the same color as his son's, were reddened by lack of sleep and worry during the last few days.

"This trip is going to be tough," Miguel said, glancing first at Luisito and then at his wife, Elena. "But many others have done it before us and we can do it too. When we get to the United States, we will be free. That is all that matters and all we need to think about right now. Okay?"

Luisito and his mother nodded.

"Sharks are my biggest worry," Elena said.

"Sharks?" Luisito said with wide-open eyes. "I had forgotten about sharks . . ."

Miguel gave Elena a stern look, shaking his head slightly.

"Hey, let's relax. Pretend we are tourists enjoying the beach at a resort," Miguel said, trying to lighten the mood. "Remember how we always wanted to go relax on those beaches like the foreign tourists, but we weren't allowed?"

"Papi, please. How did you plan this?" Luisito asked.

"It was not easy," Miguel said. "I had to wait for the right time and the right people to help us."

"I never thought it would happen," Elena said as she worked her brown hair into a ponytail, then wiped the sweat off her forehead. "Since your father is a doctor, I knew the government would make it difficult for us to leave. This is the only way we would ever be able to get off the island."

Luisito understood. Most people in Cuba were not allowed to travel freely on vacation to other countries because the government feared they would not return. Doctors especially were not allowed to leave because Cuba needed medical doctors.

"We had to make a decision soon since you are al- most of military age," Miguel said. "I knew they would draft you and who knows, maybe send you to fight in Africa. . . . Oh, let's not even think about that anymore. The worst is over."

Luisito didn't say a word, but he suspected that the worst wasn't over as the raft carried them forward into unknown waters.

✦ ✦ ✦

In the silence of the trip thoughts flooded Luisito. He replayed the last few weeks over and over in his mind, now recognizing clues to what his parents had been planning and how oblivious he had been. He remembered a few weeks ago when his neighbor, Ramon, knocked on the door late at night. His father had rushed out of bed to open the door to find Ramon with Johnny, his twenty-year-old nephew, who was visiting from the United States. The young man wore a colorful shirt with words in English, new blue jeans, and big white sneakers. *Those shoes are huge!* Luisito thought. Luisito had only seen these kinds of shoes and clothes at the *diplotienda,* a store where only the diplomats and tourists were allowed to shop. The tourists had access to another Cuba where food was not rationed in the restaurants and there were toiletry products in the hotels—a different world from the scarcity experienced by the rest of the people on the island.

Since most Cubans were barred from outside news, he had never realized how much better other people lived until the government started allowing flights from the United States. Many Cuban families who had fled Cuba before flights were restricted took this opportunity to visit their relatives. That's when Luisito started wondering why his family couldn't have soap or milk like other people.

"This is my nephew Johnny, from *La Yuma*," Ramon said that day, using the slang Cubans on the island often used to refer to the United States of America. "He brings things from your family."

The smiling young man pulled several envelopes out of a backpack that hung from his shoulders. Miguel recognized the handwriting immediately.

"It's from your cousin in Miami!" he said, turning to Elena.

Then Johnny pulled out a plastic grocery bag with a pair of glasses for Abuela, a package of soap, underwear for Luisito, and a bottle of vitamins. As he handed them the items he folded the plastic bag and was shoving it back into his backpack when Abuela stopped him.

"Wait. Can I have the plastic bag?" she asked. "Plastic bags are so hard to find. If things get really bad, I can sell it. I can get about five American dollars for this!"

"Sure," Johnny said, shrugging his shoulders and smiling. Luisito couldn't help noticing how clean this guy smelled.

Instead of reading the letters out loud, his grandmother hurried Luisito into the bathroom to use the new soap. With all his excitement over the new things, he didn't realize that his parents were reading the letters in their bedroom and speaking quietly to each other.

Luisito remembered that wonderful bath. He sure smelled terrible now! How he wished he could take a bath again. That day he turned the cold-water knob. He didn't bother to check if there was any hot water—there usually wasn't. He picked up the bar of soap and took a deep sniff. It smelled sweet. It had been three weeks since he had last used soap. He had been using water and lemons because there wasn't any soap left in the stores and his family wasn't able to purchase or barter any in *el mercado negro*, the black market. That is where many Cubans illegally bought their supplies when they had used up their allotted ration or when stores didn't have what they needed. Every store and every home was owned by the Cuban government. There was no longer any private ownership. If the stores didn't carry something, citizens had to fend for themselves.

Many more thoughts wandered through Luisito's mind as he drifted in and out of a light sleep on the raft. By now his father had turned the motor on, and they were going at a faster pace. Soon the sky turned from pitch dark to gray, and the sun began to rise. It looked as if it were coming out of the ocean and racing toward the sky. Soon it would be morning. Luisito's stomach began to rumble.

"Is there anything to eat, Papi?" he asked, trying not to sound annoying.

"*Si, hijo*, I brought some bread," Miguel said, sounding almost cheerful.

"Dip it into the water so it be easier to swallow." Miguel pointed to a bottle of water tied to the raft.

Bread was no longer made of wheat in Cuba but of yucca, a starch similar to potato. If it wasn't eaten right away the bread was hard as a rock. Luisito ate his wet bread and took a few sips of the water.

"I wonder what Mami is doing," Elena said

"She is probably at church," Luisito said, "thinking of us."

"You are probably right," Miguel said, smiling.

The hours passed but not as quickly as Luisito expected. *When there is not much to do, an hour feels like an eternity*, he thought. The weather was good and his mood was lighter. He could almost see himself arriving in the United States, the promised land. Despite his good spirits, something nagged at him: it couldn't be this easy.

# 3 TIRES

Around noon, Miguel spotted dark clouds in the sky heading straight for the raft. Luisito felt scared and helpless. There was no place to hide. He couldn't go under a bridge or down below a ship's deck. They were out in the open, just waiting for the storm to hit them.

First, the ocean became agitated. In just a few minutes, the sky grew so dark it looked like night. The wind gusted, rocking the raft like a baby's cradle. The waves came in stronger and higher every minute.

"Be careful!" Miguel repeated over and over as he held on to Luisito with one hand and the raft with the other.

"*Amparanos Señor,*" Elena prayed, imploring God to protect them, while she clutched the raft with both hands. Luisito felt so small and weak in the face of an angry Mother Nature. He did the only thing he could think of doing. He tried to repeat the prayers he used to hear Abuela say at night, but he couldn't remember them clearly.

"Our Father who art in heaven, hallowed be thy name. Hail Mary, full of grace. Please help us, *Virgen de la Caridad*!" Luisito shouted over and over the bits of prayers he could remember.

"*¡Cuidado!* Be careful. Hold on!" Miguel shouted every time a wave hit them. The hours seemed endless. Luisito hung on to the raft and tightened the muscles in his stomach to keep from throwing up as the motion made him sick.

The waves were so high that they hit Luisito and his parents in the face. It was like being slapped. Luisito tried to continue to pray. He knew there was a God somewhere. Would Abuela's God help them? Would they survive this voyage, or would they make the newspaper headlines like so many other empty rafts found on the shores without their owners?

Suddenly, as quickly as the storm had come, it began to leave. The wind ceased and the waves calmed down. The sun peeked out again from the clouds. Miguel looked around the raft, taking a quick inventory. They were alive. The raft had not been damaged, and they hadn't lost their water bottles. They did lose their loaves of bread out into the sea, but they could breathe in peace now.

"Luisito, don't worry," his mother said, reaching out to hug him. "Everything is going to be fine. The worst is over."

If only he could believe her.

Luisito lay back in the raft and closed his eyes. He thought about the storm they had just been through. What if another storm came again at night and they weren't so lucky? Poor Abuela. She was an agile seventy-two-year-old woman, but she wouldn't have survived a trip like this. Otherwise, Luisito knew, she would have escaped with them. His chest tightened and a lump formed in his throat as he pictured Abuela, who used to stand long hours in line under the hot sun waiting to get food at the grocery store. He called to mind each detail of his grandmother's tanned skin and wrinkled face.

"Do you think Abuela will be okay?" Luisito asked, breaking the silence.

"Oh, your grandmother is a woman of strong character. She will be fine," Miguel said. "As soon as we get to the United States we can worry about getting Abuela out of Cuba."

His words frightened Luisito. What would happen to Abuela if they didn't make it to the United States? He pushed those thoughts out of his head and tried to think of his dear grandmother smiling and telling him stories about the good old days. She told him stories of how middle-class Cuban families would gather socially in country clubs. There they would enjoy the beach, rent *cabanas*, and eat lunch by the ocean. Those were happy days for Elena and her parents.

Then things gradually got worse. Lusito's grandfather, Luis Jemot, was a well-known attorney in Havana. One day, two police officers came to his office to question him. They took him to a nearby prison for more questioning. Abuela was able to visit him in jail for the next few days. Then one day when she arrived, she was informed he had died suddenly of a heart attack. But other prisoners told Abuela that he had been beaten to death.

"Mami, do you think Abuela will get angry crowds in front of the house because we left?" Luisito asked. "Remember the *actos de repudio*, the group of people recruited by the government to harass those leaving Cuba? They called the *bodeguero's* son, Ivan, *gusano!*" *Gusano*, or worm, was the nickname some used to insult Cubans who wanted to leave the island.

"No, they did that to Nico, the manager of the *bodega*, to set an example since everyone knows him in the *barrio*," Miguel said, wiping the sweat from his forehead. They all nodded in agreement, falling silent. The sun hid behind the backdrop of the clouds and night fell. The stars twinkled in the most beautiful display they had ever seen. Luisito wished upon the largest one.

"What did Abuela say to you before we left?" Elena asked, interrupting Luisito's thoughts.

"A long good-bye," Luisito said, hoping his mother would not probe any further. Abuela had entrusted him with a secret. Something he must do as soon as he arrived in Florida.

# 4 CUATRO

The raft rode steadily in the morning sun. Luisito couldn't tell where the ocean ended and the sky began. He still couldn't believe this was actually happening to him. He kept thinking that maybe he would wake up soon in his sofa bed. Abuela would joke with him as she prepared his breakfast of water with sugar and some left-over bread. But no . . . even today, his desk at school would be empty. He would be marked absent, and his friends would think he was at home sick. They would never imagine he was floating on a raft in the middle of the ocean!

Luisito wondered if he would ever see his friends again. They had been such an important part of his life until only a few days ago.

Lunch and dinner came and went with nothing but water to drink. Luisito didn't feel weak, but he was very hungry.

Night fell again, and his father used a small kitchen knife to carve another line on the side of the raft to remind him of how many days they had been at sea. With the night came a steady breeze. They used the sheets to keep out the chill.

"What is that?" Luisito said as he felt a nudge on the side of the raft.

"Is it a shark?" Elena gasped, looking at Miguel.

Suddenly the creature leaped out of the water. It wasn't a shark. It was a dolphin, and as they looked even more dolphins appeared! They were all swimming in circles around the raft.

"I think they're protecting us!" Luisito smiled.

"That means there are sharks not so far away," Elena said wearily.

"Look at them, Papi!" Luisito said in amazement.

"They are really something!" Miguel replied.

After a few hours, the dolphins disappeared and Luisito fell asleep, slumped on the raft next to his mother. He hoped the dolphins were smart enough to know the sharks were gone. What if the next nudge he felt was that of a shark?

+ + +

When the sun rose the next morning it looked so close Luisito felt he could reach out and touch it from the raft. Everything seemed less frightening in the daylight. He was glad it was another day and he was still alive. They had more sips of water. He was so hungry! Suddenly, a loud screeching sound came from the motor—and then there was silence.

"What was that?" Luisito gasped.

"The motor . . . it's stopped!" his father said in a worried voice. *"¡Que barbaridad!"*

"Can we fix it, Papi?"

Miguel leaned over the side of the raft to inspect the motor. After several tense minutes he turned back to Luisito and Elena.

"The motor is very hot and I'm afraid to say it, but the motor oil has leaked out from the corroded drain plug. I see the oil floating in the water. *¡Caramba!*" he exclaimed, running his fingers through his hair. "It's ruined. I can't get it to work again!"

*"¿Ay no qué hacemos?"* said Elena. "What are we going to do?"

"Don't worry, Mami," Luisito said, holding her by the shoulders.

Miguel placed his hands on his face for a few minutes, as if thinking. Then he took a deep breath.

"Okay, no need to panic," he said. "Let's keep rowing. I had hoped the old motor wouldn't break down, but I'm prepared. I brought the oars, and as soon as there is some wind I will put up the fabric and we can sail."

Without another word, father and son began to take turns rowing. They wanted to get as far as possible during the day. Luisito rowed fast. He hadn't known he could row that fast!

"Let's not panic," Miguel said. "Slow down so you won't burn out. Keep it steady and then rest. Then you can row some more."

The sun was hotter than ever, or maybe it just felt like that because Luisito was rowing. It was burning his fair skin. His feet, too, were getting red and a bit swollen. He felt dizzy and nauseated. They fell into a rhythm of rowing and stopping at intervals to rest. Miguel took off his shirt and wet it. He handed it to Luisito.

"Here, put it on your head so you won't dehydrate," he said.

Luisito felt the cool relief of the wet shirt on his hot head. He glanced at his mother. She looked weak.

"Have some water, Mami," Luisito said, giving her the last of his water.

"No, that is for you, son," Elena said.

"No, Mami. I'm all right, please!" Luisito pleaded.

Miguel nodded at her. Elena took the water and seemed a little better.

Night fell upon them again and the chilly breeze hit Luisito. He felt sharp pains in his arms from rowing, but the mere thought of sharks and other dangers pushed him to continue.

"Don't row so fast," Miguel repeated.

Elena opened and closed her eyes as she rested, huddled on the raft. Father and son took a longer rest from rowing and drifted, letting the waves sway the raft along its way. Finally, Luisito's eyes closed and he fell asleep.

After what seemed like just a few hours, Luisito awoke to see the sun peeking out from under the clouds. There was a gentle breeze, and Miguel put up the bed sheet to use as a sail. The breeze took them swiftly along.

Then suddenly Miguel spotted something on the horizon.

"*¡Mira!* A ship!" Miguel exclaimed. They all waved their arms. Elena sat up from her crouched position and waved. The raft almost tipped over. But the ship did not appear to see them.

"*¡Aquí! ¡Aquí!*" Luisito screamed.

"*¡Miren! ¡Miren acá!*" Miguel shouted. "Please look this way!

"Over here!" Elena waved frantically.

"Can't they see us?" Miguel said.

"No! Wait!" Elena cried as the ship moved farther and farther away.

Could the crew not see them or were they ignoring them? A mix of emotions was bubbling inside the Ramirez family. Nobody said what they were all thinking: *How much longer can we survive on the open sea with no food and no water? Are we really going to make it?*

The tension that had built up inside Miguel finally came out. He buried his hands in his face and cried. Luisito could only see his father's shoulders moving up and down as he sobbed. Elena and Luisito hugged him and wept as well.

"Maybe we shouldn't have attempted this trip," Miguel said as he wiped tears from his eyes. "What have I put my family through?"

"Miguel, this was our decision," Elena said, very determined. "You know we couldn't continue living in Cuba in constant fear, at least for Luisito's sake."

Her face had more color than a few hours ago. Luisito noticed how much his mom reminded him of Abuela—beautiful and fragile but strong when she needed to be. They all sat in the raft silently, drifting without direction.

# 5 CINCO

Hours passed, or maybe they were minutes. Luisito had lost all sense of time. It was so hot. He felt dizzy and light-headed. He reached for the water container, forgetting it was empty. His heart was beating rapidly, his muscles ached from rowing, and all he could think about was cold water running down his dry throat. Suddenly, he couldn't take it any longer. He cupped his hands and reached out to drink the salty ocean water.

"No, Luisito!" Elena said.

"It will make you sick, son," Miguel said as he reached out to stop him.

"Leave me alone. I need water!" Luisito said wildly. His parents exchanged worried looks. Luisito was beginning to demonstrate the symptoms of heatstroke.

Miguel held his son back to prevent him from drinking more ocean water. He knew that his son was suffering from dehydration. He had to keep him cool without letting him drink the salty ocean water. He turned around to get his t-shirt wet and put it on Luisito's head when he heard a splash and Elena's loud gasp.

"*Ay*, Luisito!" Elena yelled, covering her face with her hands. Luisito had fallen overboard.

"Elena, help me!" Miguel shouted as he reached for his son's hands, flailing in the water.

Luisito's body was so hot from the burning sun that the warm water actually felt freezing. His feet felt too heavy to move.

"Oh, no!" he heard his mother scream repeatedly.

"Papi!" Luisito cried out as waves splashed into his mouth.

"Luisito, grab my hand!" Miguel said.

Luisito could see his father's hand like a blurry image between the waves, but each time he tried to grab it, the raft bumped into him and pushed him back.

Miguel reached for one of the oars and thrust it into the water. Luisito grabbed it and Miguel pulled him close to the raft. Then he extended his hand. Luisito felt the current push him toward the raft. He grabbed his father's fingertips.

Miguel took hold of his son by the waist and Elena helped him haul the boy into the raft. His weight almost caused it to tip over.

Both parents embraced Luisito and cried. Luisito wanted to cry, too, but for some reason tears didn't come. He kept coughing as his mother massaged his back.

"Mami . . . ," Luisito whispered.

"Don't worry, *hijo*, everything will be fine," Elena said, not believing her own words anymore.

Luisito laid his head down on the wooden surface and pressed his mother's hand. They drifted for a few more hours. They all felt emotionally drained.

"Are you feeling better?" Miguel asked Luisito later.

"I don't feel very well," Luisito replied with a helpless expression.

Then, out of nowhere, they heard a noise. It came closer and closer through the waves.

"It's a boat heading right to us!" he shouted.

"No, I can't believe it!" Elena said, weeping—this time out of joy.

Miguel frantically waved his hands, rocking the raft. Luisito weakly waved one hand, smiling at last.

"It's the U.S. Coast Guard!" said Miguel joyfully.

Luisito was too weak to get up, but his parents hugged and cried over him. The Coast Guard cutter approached them and its crew helped each one get on board. They gave the family water and warm blankets.

"Sip slowly. It might make you throw up," Elena said to Luisito when he tried to gulp down the water.

"Where are you from?" asked an officer in a white uniform who was wearing rubber gloves. "The captain of a passing cruise ship spotted your raft and called us."

"Cuba. Coming for liberty," Miguel said in broken English. Now he realized why the ship hadn't picked them up. Several other men asked them questions.

"He is not feeling very well," Elena said in Spanish, interrupting the conversation and pointing to Luisito.

"*No se preocupe*," replied one of the officers, who proceeded to take Luisito's vital signs.

"He is dehydrated. We need to get him on an IV," he said to the others.

"*¿Que dijo del niño?*" Elena said, inquiring about her son.

"He will be fine, Ma'am, don't worry," the officer told Elena in Spanish.

He then approached Miguel and asked him many questions about Cuba and about their health prior to the trip. He told the family they were about thirty miles south of Key West, Florida.

Once they reached land, an ambulance transported them to the Coast Guard station in Key West. With Luisito on a stretcher, they entered a white building, going down a long hallway and into a waiting room. Luisito observed many men and women in uniform walking up and down the hallway and into small offices. It made him nervous. He wanted to get off the stretcher.

"I am feeling better already," he said, but the officer insisted that he not walk. They found a wheelchair for Luisito and his bottle of IV fluid. He was then rolled into a small room.

Immediately, a doctor holding some files walked in. The doctor was tall and in his mid-forties. Luisito was afraid. He didn't want to be examined by a strange foreign doctor. His father had always taken care of him in Cuba. What if they gave him shots and he couldn't even ask questions because his English was not very good?

"*¿Cuantos años tienes*, Luisito?" Dr. Gonzalez asked.

"I am fourteen years old," he answered. "And you speak Spanish?"

Luisito felt suddenly at ease.

"*Si*, and I am Cuban as well," the doctor said. "Now with this IV all the fluids you lost will be replenished."

"You are Cuban?" Luisito asked.

Dr. Gonzalez told Luisito how he had left Cuba right before the revolution. His family had arrived in San Antonio, Texas, to visit an uncle who played baseball in this country. They had heard of the unrest, and his father had decided to stay a little longer. They never returned to Cuba.

"Oh, my," Luisito marveled at the thought that this doctor was Cuban and he spoke English. Luisito had heard stories from the teachers at his school that Cubans outside the island were not much better off in the United States, but Luisito saw that Dr. Gonzalez was working in this great big facility and that he had really nice shoes.

"Are they good to you here?" Luisito said, looking around the room.

"Very good, very good indeed!" The doctor smiled. "And we are going to treat you very well, too."

After Dr. Gonzalez checked Luisito, he was wheeled to another room where technicians took X-rays of his lungs and drew his blood.

"Don't worry, Luisito," the doctor said. "This is normal procedure."

His parents soon joined him. Luisito saw the bandages on their arms where their blood had been drawn, too. He watched from his room as an officer walked down the hall eating a chocolate candy bar. He stared as the officer bit into the chewy, mouth-watering sweet. Luisito knew what chocolate tasted like. He remembered the time he went to Coppelia, the ice cream parlor in Havana, on his last birthday. He had waited in line forever, but the treat was delicious!

Luisito could not believe his eyes. Abuela was right! Her stories about all the wonderful things in the United States were real! If he had gotten hold of a candy bar in Cuba, he would have taken tiny bites of it for days. At that moment, a nurse handed Luisito a bowl of soup. The warm soup coated his empty stomach and he began to feel sleepy. He felt safe at last.

# 6 SEIS

The next day, the Ramirez family were taken by bus to a refugee processing place in South Florida. The bus ride was long and the apprehension made it worse. Finally, they arrived. As they got off the bus they saw that the building was fenced in with barbed wire and there was a security guard at the entrance. It looked like a jail. Luisito stared at his parents, then looked back at the building. It was scary.

"Are we being taken to jail, Papi?" Luisito finally blurted.

"No, son," Miguel said. Then he quietly asked the officers a few questions.

"The officer has assured me that we will be fine. It's just a matter of time. They have to contact our family first," said Miguel.

"Miguel, do you believe what the officer said?" whispered Elena in a concerned tone.

"Elena, we are in the United States. Don't worry," he said.

"Well, you never know, there could be dishonest people anywhere. You can never be too sure," she said, rubbing her hands as she often did when she was nervous.

"*Mi amor*, honey, don't worry," Miguel said, holding her hand.

"Maybe we will meet someone here as nice as Dr. Gonzalez," Luisito said.

"What a set-up that was!" Miguel said, remembering the Coast Guard facility. "The medicine cabinets were full! I wish I could have had all of that at home to treat my patients."

When they entered the building, an officer approached the family and gave them bright orange uniforms. *Now we really look like prisoners*, Luisito thought. When they stepped out into the courtyard, they blended in with all the other refugees who wearily awaited news of their future. Meanwhile, immigration officials were trying to reach the Ramirezes' relatives.

As each hour passed the reality that they were in the United States started to sink in and their optimism increased. Luisito hoped that here he wouldn't go to bed hungry. And, most of all, that he could live without fear. He was buoyed by these hopes, but the memories of Abuela, his friends, and his neighborhood haunted him.

When he closed his eyes he could picture himself standing at the *Malecón*, a scenic walkway surrounding the port of Havana. He could even smell the salt water. He remembered the hills behind the rows of old houses and the shiny stars twinkling above the dark streets of his barrio. Most of all he remembered his dear Abuela's smile and her hugs. He was so happy to have escaped but, at the same time, so sad to leave all these things that had been his home.

Luisito snapped out of his memories when a cold sandwich and the most delicious apple juice were placed in front of him. There was a television set at one end of the hallway, but Luisito couldn't understand any of the programming. Cuba had been one of the first countries in Latin America to sell television sets before the revolution, but Luisito had hardly watched it on the island. First of all, they didn't have electricity most of the time. Second, the programs were all produced by the government, and they were boring. Third, if your television broke it was almost impossible to save enough money to buy another. He looked now at the TV set in the living area for the newly arrived. He was fascinated by the commercials showing all the different kinds of restaurants, instant hot soups, new toys, and new styles of clothing. Everything was so new to him!

Luisito looked around the room, which was full of adults. He then spotted another teenager with curly brown hair playing solitaire.

"¡Hola!" Luisito said.

"¡Hola!" the boy answered. Luisito was relieved that the boy spoke Spanish.

"I'm Tito," he said. "I'm from the Dominican Republic. How about you?"

"I'm Luisito from Cuba," he said.

"How did you get here?" Tito asked.

"By sea, in a raft. And you?" Luisito said.

"I came by sea as well, but in a small boat," Tito said. "How was your trip?"

"It was something, all right!" Luisito said.

"Yeah, me too," Tito said. "Here, take a seat, let me show you some card tricks."

Tito was quick with the cards in his hand. He was thirteen years old and had arrived with his mother about a month ago. Luisito hoped he didn't have to stay in this place so long. He enjoyed Tito's card tricks and his stories about growing up in the Dominican Republic.

That night, the men were taken to a locker room to shower. Then Miguel and Luisito were sent to a large room full of small beds. He slept on a cot beside his dad. His mother was taken to another room where the women slept. He hoped his mom was not worried being all by herself; he felt secure with his father.

For three days, Luisito spent his mornings in the United States being questioned in a small room with his parents. They asked him about his life in Cuba, his family, and his escape from the island. They ate in a large cafeteria. Luisito had never seen so much food in one place—and for free! During the rest of the day, he played card games with Tito and watched television, picking up some English words. Sometimes he would go where the women gathered and listen to the Spanish soap operas playing on TV. He was allowed to be with his mother. She was only away from them to shower and sleep at night.

On the fourth day, Elena's cousin Rosie arrived at the detention center. When the forty-year-old woman dressed in a nice business suit entered the room, Elena didn't recognize her immediately. She thought it was another interviewer or an immigration attorney. Elena had not seen her cousin in about twenty years.

"You don't remember me, Elenita?" Rosie said in a high-pitched voice.

"Oh, my, is it really you?" Elena exclaimed, recognizing her for the first time. "When you first walked in the door I thought it was someone else!"

Tears rolled down their cheeks as they hugged.

"You look so much prettier in person," Elena said.

"Oh, please," Rosie said, tilting her head back and laughing. "I am getting your papers ready, and in only a few more hours you will be out of here." She put an arm over Luisito's shoulder.

"You are tall! You take after your father," she said, looking at Miguel, who gave her a hug. "We will be going straight to the airport and flying to Maryland, where the whole family is waiting for you."

Maryland! That was news that Luisito was not expecting. He had to carry out Abuela's instructions in Miami, at the shrine of Our Lady of Charity. What was he going to do now?

"Can we stay in Miami for a day or two?" Luisito asked.

"I'm afraid not," Rosie said. "I have to be back in Maryland for work, but I will take vacation soon and we can visit with my parents in Miami."

Rosie moved her hands quickly while she spoke. Luisito observed her long red fingernails and the clicking of her charm bracelet. She had a wedding ring with a sparkling diamond, something Luisito had never seen before.

"I brought some warm sweaters for you in the car. You might be chilly on the plane ride to Maryland," she said.

"But can we visit the shrine of Our Lady of Charity before we take off?" Luisito insisted.

"Why?" Elena said. "How do you know about that?" His parents looked at each other in amazement. They had never spoken to him about the shrine.

"Abuela told me about it," Luisito said.

"*Ay, el niño* wants to pray there?" Rosie said, looking at his parents with a tender smile. "Oh, he is such a good boy. Of course, you want to visit the shrine of Our Lady of Charity, the patron of Cuba, to thank her for your arrival. But there is not much time before our flight back. Maybe we can all come for Christmas."

Luisito wanted to explain his urgency but he couldn't. It was Abuela's strict instruction not to mention anything to anyone. His parents might not approve.

Meanwhile, Luisito went to the main hall to say good-bye to Tito.

"I am getting out of here!" he said.

"*Buena suerte*!" Tito said, giving Luisito a pat in the back. "I hope I can get out of here myself."

Tito smiled genuinely, but with a trace of sadness since his own destiny was still in question and he was now losing his new friend.

Luisito gave him a piece of paper with his soon-to-be address in Baltimore, Maryland.

"Keep warm! I hear it gets cold in Maryland," Tito said, giving Luisito another quick pat on the shoulder.

"I will try!" Luisito smiled.

# 7 SIETE

A few hours later, the Ramirezes took off their orange uniforms and changed into clothes Rosie
had brought them. Luisito felt good taking off the orange
jumpsuit. He quickly changed into a red shirt with a little
animal on the chest. He couldn't see exactly what it was.
A frog perhaps? He looked at himself in the bathroom
mirror. No, it was an alligator! He then climbed into a
pair of blue jeans and pulled on a brown sweater.

A red car awaited them outside the center, and, to
their surprise, Rosie's elderly parents were there to greet
them. They were the only close relatives the Ramerizes
had in Miami.

"*¡Muchacho!* So many years without seeing you!" said Rosie's father, Manuel, a strong seventy-year-old.

"I am so happy to see you!" said Rosie's mom, Maria Cristina, who was affectionately called Maricusa. She was Abuela's only sister.

"I like living in Florida where it is warm," Maricusa said, smiling. "They are young," she said, pointing to her daughter. "They can deal with the cold winters. Anyway, they visit every summer and for Christmas."

Luisito was relieved that he could come for Christmas. That was only six months away. He still had time to fulfill his promise to Abuela.

Maricusa seemed to Luisito like a younger version of Abuela. He felt a little cheated because they had only just met and now he had to leave for the airport. He wished he could stay a while longer.

"Too bad this is so quick," said Manuel, Rosie's father, as if he were reading Luisito's mind. "It would have been great to have you here a few days, but I understand that you need to settle things quickly in Maryland with school starting soon."

"We will come up for Christmas this year," Maricusa said. "And that way we will see the whole family and have a snowy Christmas!"

"I want to come to Miami for Christmas," Luisito said, looking around for acknowledgement.

"Christmas is much prettier up north with all the snowmen and pine trees decorated," Rosie said.

"Well, we'd better get going," said Manuel, looking at this watch. Luisito squeezed into the backseat with his mother, Rosie, and Maricusa. The vinyl seats of the red Impala seemed as hot as the sun itself. His dad sat in the front with Manuel as they drove to the security checkpoint. Manuel gave the security guard some papers and then got out and opened the trunk. The guard looked inside and gestured that they could leave.

Luisito felt a huge sense of relief as the car drove away from the barbed-wired, prisonlike detention center. He pressed his face on the glass as they drove through a neighborhood. He noticed with amazement that every house had a car, and some had more than one. He also observed that the houses were all painted and that none of them had poles on the sides holding them up like in his hometown.

During the drive to the airport, Elena and Miguel continued retelling their escape, while Luisito interrupted with his own comments.

"You should have seen us rowing that tiny raft," said Luisito.

"You were very lucky to have survived the trip without any major storms. It's the beginning of hurricane season!" Rosie said.

"If you went back you would not even recognize your birthplace," Elena said, whispering as she did in Cuba for fear of being heard.

"You can't trust anyone," Miguel added. "You don't know who will snitch on you."

Finally, after several ramps and turns, they were at the airport terminal. They piled out of the car, exchanging many hugs and good-byes, and promising to return to visit Maricusa and Manuel. Rosie's luggage was turned over to a clerk at the airline booth. Luisito was amazed at all the different people he saw and the way they were dressed. Teenagers were reading colorful magazines. Three children played with something in a box. The oldest boy looked about twelve years old. He carried the box and all the others talked to it. Luisito was curious as to what animal was in there.

He overheard the family speaking in Spanish, although they had an accent he had not heard before. The kids spoke in English among themselves.

"*¡Mira!*" said the boy, pointing to the box he held in his hands.

"*Si*, what is it?" Luisito asked. He stared into a box but saw only a stone.

"It's my new pet rock," said the boy, smiling.

"What is the boy saying?" Elena asked Luisito.

"He said that's his pet rock," Luisito whispered to his mother, and he rolled his eyes.

"Oh, how unusual. Stay close to us, Luisito," she said nervously.

They walked down a long hall until they reached a row of what looked like movie theater seats.

"When are we ever getting on the plane?" Luisito asked.

"Oh, but we are on the plane, Luisito," Rosie said, smiling.

"What do you mean? How did I get on?"

"You didn't realize it, but when we were walking down the hall we were getting on the plane," Rosie explained. "Here, push up the window shade so you can see the takeoff."

Luisito had never been on a plane before. He was a little scared at first. However, it all seemed much safer than the raft he had been on. After some chatting, three packs of peanuts, and two sodas, Luisito landed at Baltimore-Washington International Airport with his family.

# 8 OCHO

Relatives and friends greeted them at the airport with posters and bouquets of flowers. Luisito was blinded by camera flashes. Women of all shapes and sizes hugged him and pinched his cheeks. Men greeted him with pats on the head and slaps on the back. There were hugs and tears all the way to the parking lot. Instant cameras spit out green pictures that were fanned until dry to produce images of his family.

Luisito never realized he had so much family! Back in Cuba, there were only his parents and Abuela. No one else. He was now part of a clan with many kids his own age! Rosie introduced him to each family member and explained how they were related. It was too much information at once, so Luisito decided that for now he would just smile and nod. Finally, he was introduced to Rosie's husband, José, son, Tommy, and daughter, Sonia.

José was tall and muscular with premature gray in his hair that complemented his youthful face. He spoke some Spanish but much more English. He said he came from Cuba when he was five years old. He had a contagious laugh and a carefree attitude. He mentioned that he was an architect and had designed his own house. Luisito had never really thought of anyone doing such a thing. The only construction projects he knew of in Cuba were the hotels built by foreigners.

Luisito observed how the luggage swirled by and passengers would quickly pick them up. *How could they tell which was theirs*, Luisito thought, when all the luggage looked the same to him? During the car ride to Rosie's home, the adult conversation revolved around the different ways Abuela could legally come to the United States. Luisito listened quietly for about an hour, until they arrived at a house with a well-manicured lawn. More people came out the door to greet them, many of them women who bore a resemblance to his Abuela. Some of them snapped pictures; others were too busy hugging to remember to take pictures.

When Luisito entered Rosie's house, a rich blend of seasonings in the air greeted him. He followed the pleasant aromas to the kitchen, where pots and pans were full of good things to eat. He watched as busy hands cut up vegetables and sprinkled spices for salads, sauces, and stews. Luisito couldn't believe so much food could exist in one single home. There were foods he had never seen or eaten before! He wondered if they worked for the government. Then he remembered things were different in this country. Back in Cuba, only those in the military or who were well connected had access to these things.

"Luisito, *con esa pinta vas a tener a las muchachas así,*" some of the elderly relatives teased him.

Luisito noticed that some of his girl cousins laughed or rolled their eyes at the men's silly remarks about having several girlfriends at a time.

"Don't listen to them, Luisito," Rosie said, laughing. "They are married to their only girlfriends!"

"I know," Luisito said laughing. *"Perro que ladra no muerde."*

Everyone laughed at the old Spanish saying that literally says a barking dog doesn't bite, meaning that those who talk a lot are just bluffing.

"Here, taste this, Luisito; does it need more salt?" asked a relative stirring something on the stove. The creamy sauce filled Luisito's mouth and he licked his lips with delight.

Relatives were turning Luisito this way and that. He was being hugged, patted on the head, and introduced to more cousins his age.

*"¡Los primos!"* they shouted. He never knew he had so many cousins! They all waved shyly. Luisito found their names so strange and hard to pronounce: Sean, Avery, Ashley, Bradley. He wasn't sure if the names were for boys or girls when he heard them in conversation. It was incredible for him to think that he had family that spoke a different language, with a completely different lifestyle, and yet with some similar customs.

# 9 NUEVE

There was a tender *lechón asado* with rice and black beans, fried plantains, *yucca* with *mojito*, soft warm Cuban bread, and salad set on the table. On the side there was a smaller tray with slices of lean turkey, stuffing, and the creamy gravy he had tasted earlier. For dessert, they had a choice of flan with shredded coconut or chocolate cake with ice cream.

He looked at his parents, who were staring at all the food on the table. Luisito knew what they were probably thinking. Their thoughts were back in Cuba at the empty tables of friends and of Abuela that very evening.

The conversation went on through the night while photo albums were passed around and the smell of Cuban coffee filled the room. Rosie's two-story house was too big for her family of four, Luisito thought. He wondered where he would sleep. For now, he enjoyed watching his parents smile as they spoke with the family.

In the living area, there was a big stone fireplace, and Luisito wondered if they ever cooked on it when the electricity went out. He wanted to ask all the questions that popped into his mind as he glanced around the room, but everyone was talking at the same time. He could barely hear his own thoughts.

Then out of a big *escaparate*, a wooden armoire like the ones Luisito's parents used as closets in Cuba, a huge TV screen appeared.

"Look at this, guys," José said, proudly pointing a small box directly at the TV. "Did you see that?"

"What?" said Ramon, an elderly uncle.

"Don't look at me," José said. "Look what happens to the TV set."

"Wow!" said some of the younger kids.

"It turns on and off without having to get up," José said, smiling.

"These Americans are incredible! Look what they have invented," Ramon marveled.

"It's called a *clicker*," José said.

"Dad, that was ages ago. My teacher calls it a remote," said Tommy.

As if by magic, the remote not only turned the TV on and off and made it louder and quieter, but it also changed the channels. And the TV set was in color!

"He has always liked technology. He always buys the newest thing on the market," said Adita, José's mother.

"His father was like that, too—we were one of the first families to have a black-and-white TV in Cuba, before the revolution."

The adult family members gathered around as the younger crowd squatted on the floor to watch TV.

"Your son is so happy," an aunt who was sitting on the sofa said to Elena.

"I am happy," Luisito answered, patting his stomach. *"¡Barriga llena corazón contento!"*

Everyone laughed except some of the younger cousins, and Tommy looked puzzled. They couldn't understand Luisito's rhyming proverbs and his fast-spoken Spanish.

Tommy was Luisito's age, thin like Luisito but with brown hair cut short and spiked. Subtly, Tommy asked his older sister, Sonia, what Luisito had just said.

"He said, 'full stomach, happy heart,'" Sonia answered. "It's a Spanish proverb. Maybe he can teach you some Cuban culture."

"You think you are all that because you know more Spanish than me, but you know what?" Tommy paused dramatically, ready to supply some proverbs himself. "It's better to catch two birds in a bush, with just one stone."

"Oh, boy," Sonia said, rolling her eyes. "Try again!"

# 10 DIEZ

Later, after much talk, the relatives began to excuse themselves for the evening.

"Stay a little longer," Rosie pleaded.

"We have work tomorrow," some of the men said. Or, "It's a long drive back home."

"*El que madruga Dios lo ayuda*, right, Luisito?" one uncle said.

*God helps those who rise early.* It was as if he was dueling Luisito with another proverb.

"*Si, pero,*" Luisito said, holding up his index finger as if he was about to recite a poem, "*no hagas como el apóstol trece, que come y desaparece.*"

"Luisito!" Elena nudged him. "He is always joking."

"What did he say?" a young cousin asked her mother.

"He said not to be like the thirteenth apostle, who ate and left," her mother said laughing.

"*Oye*, I am going to call you Luisito, *el rey de los dichos*," Tommy said, laughing. "Luisito, the king of the proverbs. It even rhymes in Spanish!"

The crowd laughed as they walked outside. There was another round of kisses and hugs, and finally cars started driving away.

Luisito was amazed to see that everyone had a new-looking car. In Cuba, there were no new cars. People could not afford them. Most people didn't have a car and those that did drove the old cars they had before the existing government took power. The Ramirez family had owned only one car that had belonged to Luisito's maternal grandfather, Luis. His dad used that car to get to the hospital. To make ends meet, his father also used the car as a taxi for tourists on his days off. The government didn't approve of this type of private business, but officials looked the other way since the car was also used as an ambulance on many occasions.

Since they didn't have an extra car, Elena, who had worked in a day care center, left at five in the morning to stand at the corner of *La Avenida Del Presidente* with several neighbors until a government sixteen-wheeler truck passed by and gave them a ride to work. These trucks were used for public transportation because most of the buses were broken, overcrowded, or not running because of the gas shortage.

Sleepily Luisito walked into the now quiet house with his parents and Rosie's family. The two-story home that had been bustling with noise and energy now seemed eerily quiet.

"I have set you up to sleep tonight in the basement," Rosie said to Miguel and Elena. "Luisito, you can sleep in your own room in the basement or you can share Tommy's room."

Luisito didn't know what to say. He had never had a room of his own. It would be great to have so much space to himself. On the other hand, he had never had a brother, and sharing a room could be fun.

"Mom, I thought he was sharing my room?" Tommy said quickly.

"Luisito, would you like that?" Rosie asked.

"Sure, great!" Luisito said, smiling.

"Come on, let's go!" Tommy gestured toward Luisito.

The house seemed so big that Luisito wished he had a map. He looked around and imagined how many families would live in a house this size in Cuba. There were stairs to go up and stairs to go down. He soon learned that the downstairs was the basement. It was a whole apartment and colder than the rest of the house! It had a living room, a small kitchen, and two bedrooms. The first floor contained the large living area, the kitchen, the dining room, three bedrooms, and two bathrooms.

Luisito thought this was all there was to the house, but there was more: a laundry area and a staircase that led to the attic, which was furnished with a desk and two bookcases. A model train that Tommy had built with his dad several Christmases ago was set up on the floor. There was also a telescope that the boys looked through to see a beautiful sky filled with stars, just as in Cuba.

Luisito couldn't wait to write to Abuela and tell her all the things he was discovering.

"Papi and I come here the most. This is our space," Tommy said.

Although Luisito had only taken English as a school subject and never really practiced it, he started finding he could understand more than he thought.

"*¡Que bien!*" Luisito said.

"Tommy, you can show him the train set tomorrow. Now it is time to rest," Rosie called, and the boys came downstairs and settled into their room.

Luisito looked around Tommy's room at all the large posters of the American football stars and pictures of big dolphins everywhere.

"You sure like fish!" Luisito said, smiling.

Tommy proudly picked up a football helmet and showed it to Luisito.

"That's not just any fish—that's the Miami Dolphins mascot, silly!" he said, laughing. The boys laughed and talked awhile longer, repeating phrases and often gesturing with their hands.

Luisito lay down in his new bed—the most comfortable he had ever slept in. He pulled a fluffy blanket over himself. Luisito was not used to air conditioning. He closed his eyes and thought that from now on he would never wake up all sweaty from the heat of those Havana summer nights. This was the life!

Then a sudden feeling of guilt overwhelmed him as he realized that his Abuela would have to sweat tonight in her bed. She would probably be scared to open the window since she would be all alone in the apartment. He tossed and turned a few times. Abuela had entrusted him with a special mission. He had to get to Miami soon and relay his message to a particular priest there. He repeated Abuela's message over and over in his head. He was afraid he might forget it, but he was more afraid to write it down for fear someone would read it. He couldn't make anything out of her message, but the Cuban priest Abuela told him he should speak to at the shrine would know what to do. Abuela's older brother, Tío César, had been a priest in Cuba for many years before his death. Abuela had many connections with the Cuban clergy. *This priest must be someone she knows very well,* Luisito thought. He hoped he could persuade his family to go to Miami for Christmas.

# 11 ONCE

The next morning Luisito woke up ready for breakfast. He looked at Tommy's bed, but Tommy was already gone. Someone had left a t-shirt and a pair of shorts beside his bed. Luisito put them on and hurried down the stairs. He didn't know which way to go, so he began opening doors.

The first was a bathroom, then a laundry room with two big machines and several brooms and mops. Then he saw Tommy on the other side of the hallway.

"*Oye*, I thought you would never wake up!" Tommy said.

"Am I late for breakfast?" Luisito said.

"Breakfast! It's lunchtime," Tommy said, smiling. "Come on, my mom is grilling hamburgers outside."

Luisito followed Tommy out to the patio. The grown-ups were sitting on the patio furniture and Sonia was now turning the hamburgers on the grill. Tommy had told Luisito that she was seventeen years old. She was wearing a t-shirt that didn't quite reach her waist, jogging pants, and flip-flops. Luisito remembered that in Cuba, many girls had flip-flops because they couldn't buy shoes and their t-shirts were too small. If they only knew that in the United States it was fashion.

"*¡Oye, dormilón!*" Miguel called to his son.

"Sleepyhead! That's what my dad calls me, too," said Tommy.

"How does it feel to wake up in America?" José said, smiling.

"Great!" Luisito beamed.

"Before you know it he is going to be speaking English fluently and he will be a little *Americanito*," Rosie joked.

Sonia handed Luisito a glass of milk and a hamburger, and he watched as his cousins poured some tomato sauce called *ketchup* all over their hamburgers. Luisito copied them. It occurred to Luisito that if he had to ask for food in this country he wouldn't even know what to call it. In Cuba, he had mostly eaten rice, beans, and eggs.

"We are going to take you today to visit the Baltimore waterfront," Rosie said. "Would you like that?"

"I don't really want to see any more water," Luisito said.

"I understand," Rosie smiled. "How about if you go to the movies with Sonia and Tommy while I take your mom to the store to buy some clothes for you all?"

"You can sit close to me and I will translate," Sonia said. "We can go see an action movie—that way I don't have to translate too much!"

They all laughed. Luisito didn't really care what movie they went to see because everything was a new adventure. He took another bite of his hamburger and realized that he wasn't too fond of this ketchup invention. He leaned back on his chair underneath the blue-and-white patio umbrella. For the second time in his life, his stomach was full and he was content.

"Eat, Elenita," Rosie said gesturing toward the hamburgers. "You hardly ate."

"I can't eat," Elena said.

"We were just talking about that last night," Miguel explained. "It is hard to eat so much knowing Abuela and our friends in Cuba have so little."

"I understand," José said.

"Well, let's talk about Luisito's new school," Rosie said, changing the subject. "I took a week off so I can help you get the paperwork for working permits and get Luisito settled in school. We could combine the things we need to do with some sightseeing. There are many historical places here we could show you."

"Let's take him to the Smithsonian Museum in Washington!" Tommy said.

"We'll think about it," Rosie said, smiling. "Now, off to the movies with you! Oh, and Sonia, stop at the grocery store on your way, please. We've run out of shredded coconut for our famous flan."

Sonia was all smiles as the three drove off in her small candy red car. She spoke Spanish with a heavy American accent and used many hand gestures to explain things to Luisito.

When they arrived at the supermarket, Luisito was stunned. It was like a fairy tale! As by magic, the door opened by itself! He walked into a large warehouse full of food—more than he had ever seen—and people were taking loads of it in little carts to their cars.

Were they looting? Were they allowed to take all this food home? There were no lines outside the store, and inside there were aisles and aisles of all sorts of foods to buy. He picked up a banana and was about to peel it when Sonia warned him.

"Oh, no, we must pay first," she explained.

"Oh," Luisito said feeling a little embarrassed as he carried the banana with him to the register. Bananas and oranges were the only fruits he recognized from the piles of many-colored fruits displayed in the produce section.

Sonia picked a large can of shredded coconut. Luisito could not believe anyone could just pick one item from this huge supermarket. He would spend hours buying all sorts of things here.

He only wished he had more time to look at all the items in the store, especially all the candy by the register, but the line moved so quickly he didn't have a chance. He was so happy he couldn't stop smiling. He noticed no one else seemed to smile as they waited in line. He would ask his relatives to bring him back to this grocery some other day.

While they waited in line, Sonia picked up a chocolate candy bar and a glossy magazine. Luisito flipped through the pages filled with pictures of boys and some pretty girls who were all unknown to him. Sonia smiled and said something to the boy who was putting the items in the bag. Then she waved back at him with her free hand. He had his hair parted in the middle and layered to the side. Luisito looked at the magazine and back at the boy at the cash register. He looked just like some of the guys in the magazine! As Sonia walked out, the boy at the register glanced at her shoes and made some comment. She laughed and moved her shoe back and forth so he could see them better. The bottoms of her shoes were *see-through* plastic. The boy flashed a peace sign with two fingers in a V, and she did the same back to him. What a strange greeting, Luisito thought.

Sonia took the candy bar she had just purchased from the grocery bag and handed it to Luisito.

"You don't need to show the booklet?" Luisito asked Sonia. He was referring to the ration booklet all Cubans have to show back on the island. The booklet gives families permission to buy certain items monthly or yearly.

"What booklet?" laughed Sonia.

"Nothing," he said, smiling.

Luisito wished he could call Abuela right now and tell her what he had seen and how right she had been. What seemed to be fairy tales were now becoming believable to Luisito. He had a feeling he was going to like this country very much!

When Sonia, Tommy, and Luisito arrived at the movie theater, Sonia groaned.

"What's wrong?" Luisito said.

"Look at the line!" she said.

Luisito saw a few people in line to buy tickets, and he could not understand what the fuss was all about. In Cuba, the lines to get bread went down the block.

"Oh, come on, that is nothing," Luisito laughed. "Let's get in line. *Perro que no anda no encuentra hueso.*"

"A dog that does not go out does not find the bone. What in the world does that mean?" Tommy asked.

"It means you can't succeed if you don't try," Luisito said, laughing. "I am going to have to write these down for you."

"You bet," Tommy teased. "I am going to have to carry them in my pocket like a tourist with a dictionary."

As his cousins bought tickets, Luisito looked at the marquee and the upcoming movie posters. *How could anyone choose?* he thought.

"Nothing really good," Sonia said, as she eyed the signs. Luisito laughed.

"What?" Sonia said, grinning.

They bought popcorn, chocolate candy, and some water. They walked into a cool, dark movie theater and sat eating until the movie began.

There was not much need for translating. The hero in the movie didn't talk very much. He did a lot of shooting and rescued some prisoners at the end, which caused the audience to cheer.

As they walked out Luisito kept inhaling the wonderful popcorn smell.

"Popcorn actually smells better than it tastes," Luisito declared with a deep breath.

"I've never thought about it," Tommy said, taking a long sniff. "But I think you're right."

"Come on, you two," Sonia said. "People are watching. They are going to think you are *locos en la cabeza*."

They laughed as they looked for the car in the vast parking lot.

"Let's go back home and team up with Mom," Sonia said. "Maybe they already returned from their shopping and are planning something else."

# 12 DOCE

_E_arly the next morning, Rosie had planned another outing. Luisito helped José pack the car
with some coolers.

"Are we going to a grocery store today?" Luisito
asked eagerly.

"Nooo . . . ," Tommy said, glancing at his father and
rolling his eyes. "What is it with you and grocery stores?"

"We are taking you to Emmitsburg to the shrine of
Saint Elizabeth Ann Seton," José said.

"Since the first time I visited Emmitsburg, I prayed
constantly to this saint so that you could safely get out of
Cuba some day," Rosie said, smiling as she sat in the car.
"She is the first American-born saint."

"Really? Well, let's go!" Luisito said, thinking that visiting a church would remind him of his dear Abuela.

When they arrived an hour and a half later, Rosie pulled a cooler out of the trunk. She passed out drinks and *pan con timba*.

"Oh, my!" Elena said, putting her hands over her mouth. "I haven't had *pan con timba* since I was a little girl!"

"What is it?" Luisito wanted to know.

"It's a sandwich of Cuban bread with sweet guava and cream cheese," said Miguel, taking a bite from his sandwich and closing his eyes while enjoying the taste.

"This bread is delicious!" Luisito said as he tried it. "Remember back home how hard our bread was? Is this Cuban bread?"

"I couldn't find Cuban bread here in Maryland, but I improvised with this other bread," Rosie said.

"Look, up in the air!" Sonia pointed.

"It's beautiful," Luisito said. In the midst of the perfect blue sky, in between the Catoctin Mountains, appeared a gold statue of the Blessed Mother as the Immaculate Conception.

"There's a seminary there and the loveliest replica of the grotto of Lourdes in France," José said.

"What gardens they have!" said Rosie. "We will show you on another visit."

"Oh, my . . ." Elena said. "My mother was so fond of the Blessed Mother, especially *la Caridad del Cobre*."

If there is anything about religion that Luisito knew, it was *la Virgen de la Caridad del Cobre*, Our Lady of Charity. In 1612, three young men were caught in a storm in the Bay of Nipe in Cuba. They turned to prayer, and they felt their prayers answered when they saw a beautiful doll-like statue appear floating in the water. The image appeared on a wooden tablet that read, *"Yo Soy La Virgen de la Caridad,"* meaning: "I am the Virgin of Charity." The farmers were amazed that the image was not wet or spoiled by the rough seas. They brought the statue to shore and built a beautiful shrine for Mary in the city of El Cobre in the province of Oriente, Cuba. In 1916, Pope Benedict XV declared her the patroness of Cuba. The original image remains at the shrine of El Cobre.

Anyone and everyone knew *La Virgencita*, another of the many names for the Blessed Mother. She was a cultural icon on the island. Even those who didn't know much about being Catholic knew exactly who she was and how she had appeared in Cuban waters. She was an important part of the mission Abuela had entrusted to Luisito.

Luisito wanted to ask more questions, but everyone had finished eating and seemed eager to visit the Basilica of Saint Elizabeth Ann Seton.

When Luisito entered the museum, he was mesmerized to see the belongings of an actual saint in glass-covered exhibits just like the museums of patriots in Cuba. He looked at the saint's wedding ring displayed along with her father's medicine bag. It looked as old as his father's medicine bag back on the island.

"Look, Papi, like your bag," Luisito said, pointing at the glass case.

He asked Sonia and Tommy to translate many of the explanations under the glass coverings.

"She had five kids before she was widowed," Rosie said.

"She definitely was a saint!" Elena said, laughing.

The family had fun reading about and seeing the things that had belonged to Saint Elizabeth. Luisito's attention was drawn to a large framed picture of Jesus crucified that had hung in Mother Seton's bedroom. It was her favorite picture. Luisito remembered something Abuela had said years ago. She had pointed to a crucifix and said that the Lord had been crucified for teaching things which had angered some of the leaders of his time. Since then the picture of Jesus reminded him of Cubans. It reminded him of people like his grandfather, beaten and tortured to death without ever committing a crime.

Then they walked toward the basilica. Luisito saw a man take his picture. He looked around and saw another man walking behind him; he must have been the one the man was photographing. The men walked away quickly, which Luisito found strange. He had to remind himself he was not in Cuba and he had no reason to feel frightened.

Saint Elizabeth's remains were buried under a side marble altar in a large, impressive church. The church reminded Luisito of the times he had accompanied Abuela to Mass. He couldn't remember the actual Mass, but he remembered the beautiful statues, the smell of the smoldering candles, and the music. His grandmother went to Mass every Sunday regardless of the possible consequences.

Luisito had accompanied her until he was about six years old. Then one Monday morning in school his teacher asked the class how many of them had attended Mass. Luisito and two other girls raised their hands. The teacher made them stand in front of the class.

"You are so silly," she said. "Put out your hands."

The kids did as they were told. Luisito was afraid he had done something wrong and was going to get slapped with a ruler.

"Now, ask God to give you candy. Come on, pray!" the teacher demanded.

Luisito and the other girls just stood there without saying a word.

"Come on, close your eyes and pray!" the teacher said in an angry tone.

"Now, open your eyes," she said mockingly. "Do you see any candy?"

Luisito and the girls looked at their empty hands.

"Now, close your eyes and ask the government for candy!" She laughed as she placed candy in their hands. "It's the government you should always trust!"

When Luisito came home and told the story his parents were horrified.

"Well, tell that teacher that my hand is extended and I want food. How come the government doesn't come over here and give it to me!" Abuela had said, indignant. "Even better, why doesn't the government let me make money of my own instead of controlling my life!"

"Mami, don't say that to Luisito. He might repeat it and then we will all be in big trouble." Elena had said.

"It's best he doesn't go back to Mass. We have enough problems!" Miguel decided. That was the last time Luisito ever went to church with Abuela, although he would often hear her praying quietly in the evenings.

Luisito felt a sense of peace in this church. It was so quiet and beautiful. His parents knelt and prayed by

Mother Seton's side altar. Tears were rolling down their cheeks. He could see his dad's shoulders moving up and down as he buried his face in his hands. It had been many years since they had stepped inside a church. Finally, they got up and wiped their tears and hugged each other. Elena and Miguel walked outside the church into the beautiful sunny day. Everything in this country looked different to Luisito. It was like the memories of the island were in black and white and everything he saw in the United States was clean, new, bright, and colorful—just like his mood.

# 13 TRECE

Meanwhile, in Havana, Abuela sat in her rocking chair and prayed the rosary. The white beads of her rosary passed gently through her fingers as she fervently prayed each Hail Mary. She had first prayed incessantly for the safe arrival of her family, and now she prayed that she could be reunited with them soon. Those first anxiety-ridden days, knowing her family was out at sea risking their lives, kept her from any sleep. She had consoled so many women who had come to church crying desperately because their families had been lost at sea. For one long week, she had been in their shoes, pacing around her small apartment alone, praying to God that they would make it all right.

As planned, the day after her family had left, she burst into the police headquarters pretending she didn't know where they had gone.

"Please, tell me. What have you done with them?" she asked the young man in a military uniform, who had no idea what she was talking about.

"My daughter, her husband, and my grandson have disappeared!" Abuela said frantically. "They couldn't have all disappeared at the same time. The government must be questioning them somewhere, but why?" she begged to know.

Abuela hated how the government forced families to lie just to survive, just as she was lying right now. Cubans had to lie every day about their true feelings. They even had to steal food to survive. Many shop owners and farmers secretly separated a small stash of items for themselves and their family or to sell in the black market before they gave their crops to the government.

Then Abuela received a call from Maricusa, her sister, in Miami.

"*¡Hola!* Maria Elena," Maricusa said. "You wouldn't believe what I am going to tell you, but your family is here in Florida! What a surprise we had when the Coast Guard called us!"

Abuela chose her words carefully. "*¡No me digas!* I have been scared to death not knowing where they were," Abuela said as rehearsed, knowing that her phone call might be overheard. "How could they possibly leave me here alone without family?"

"Well, Maria Elena, you know how young people are, but please don't be too hard on them when they call you.

They are en route to Maryland," Maricusa said, sounding giddy with happiness.

Then Abuela heard static in their phone line, and she knew the conversation was going to be cut off. What a bad actress her sister had been. *She would have never survived in this communist Cuba*, Abuela thought.

"Thank you for calling, Maricusa!" Abuela said very solemnly. Then when she hung up, she looked at her ceiling and thanked the Lord. She felt like dancing all around the empty apartment. They had made the dangerous voyage and survived! She had to remember to control her happiness so her neighbors would not hear her bursting into laughter and shrieks of joy.

# 14CATORCE

Luisito was very tired from all the sightseeing in Maryland. He slept heavily, but woke up suddenly in the middle of the night, opening his eyes and looking around for Abuela. He had shared the living room with Abuela for so many years. He could just imagine she was there beside him as he lay in bed. He finally fell back to sleep. Hours later, he woke up to a strange noise that sounded like frogs croaking. He jumped out of bed only to discover that it was Tommy's alarm clock.

He knew he would be going shopping with his mother and Rosie for school clothes this morning. He was excited. He rushed to the living room.

"Hey, Tommy, you want to come? I am going shopping," Luisito said excitedly.

"Heck, no!" Tommy said. "I hate shopping! Then I have to help carry all the shopping bags. That's all right. I will stay home and watch TV."

Did he say *all those shopping bags*? Luisito thought. What a great day!

Luisito wolfed down his breakfast of toast with butter and *café con leche* and joined Rosie, his mother, and Sonia in the car.

"Come on, Luisito. The stores are just around the corner," Rosie said. But Luisito figured that in Maryland around the corner meant at least a thirty-minute ride.

The stores were nothing like Luisito imagined.

"Is this just one store?" Luisito asked.

"No, there are many stores in this one building. It is called a mall," Rosie explained. "It's better this way because you can walk inside without dealing with the hot or cold weather."

They entered through the perfume department. There were so many different smells that it drove Luisito crazy. His mother tried on many different perfumes. She looked like a kid in a toy store. Luisito wanted to leave this part of the store before he spent the whole day smelling like a girl!

Then they stepped onto the escalator to the second floor. Luisito pretended he wanted to see something downstairs again so he could ride on it one more time!

"This reminds me of *El Encanto*," Elena said. "It was a beautiful store in Cuba before the revolution. It sold items from Europe and from the United States."

"From the United States?" Sonia said, surprised.

"Yes, and what a store it was!" Elena said. "There were such helpful employees who had been working there for years and knew so much about their products. The items you purchased were often delivered to your house."

"I remember *El Encanto*, as well," Rosie said joining in the nostalgia. "A few days before we left Cuba my mother took me to buy a coat. You could see that many shelves were empty. It was evident that things were going downhill in our country."

As the foursome walked around the store, a man in his thirties, blond and wearing a t-shirt and jeans, watched them from afar. At first, Elena didn't pay any attention. Then the same feeling she had in Cuba came back to her. She realized that the man, who was pretending to look at the merchandise, was also keeping a steady eye on them. The man glanced at two other men a few yards behind Elena. These men had dark hair and looked Hispanic. They wore checkered shirts, dark slacks, and black shoes. Was something going on between them? She had seen those two men at the perfume stand.

Luisito also noticed the men. Were they all together? Were they planning to mug them? The two dark-haired men pretended to read the label on a box of men's slippers, but the box was upside-down. When they saw that they had been noticed they turned around and left quickly. *These men look familiar—but that couldn't be possible,* Luisito thought. He had only been in this country for a few weeks.

The blond man watched the two men leave, and he continued to keep an eye on Luisito and his family.

"I think that guy likes you, Sonia," Luisito said. "He keeps glancing this way."

Sonia smiled at Luisito and twirled her hair.

"How can anyone resist?" she said jokingly and then looked in the general direction of the guy. "Eww, he is ugly!" she said.

*"Niña, que te oye,"* her mother said, reprimanding her for saying that out loud.

"I am not rude. He is the one staring," she said turning around.

"Kids!" her mother said, rolling her eyes and smiling at Elena.

Elena continued to have an uneasy feeling but she dismissed it as a result of having lived so many years in constant fear. They continued shopping and the man kept his distance. At a certain point they realized he had disappeared as well.

Rosie bought Luisito several pair of jeans, shirts, shorts, long pants, one nice, dressy, black pair of shoes, and a pair of sneakers. They also bought a dark blue coat, mittens, and a cap for the winter. Then they purchased a few items and a coat for Elena as well. Miguel had been shopping the day before with José to buy clothes for work.

After they left the mall, Rosie took them for lunch at another restaurant where they ate hamburgers. *Apparently a common dish in this country*, Luisito thought.

When they sat down they saw the same young man who had been following them sitting in a corner booth eating a burger.

"Isn't that the blond guy from the store?" Luisito asked.

"Well, this restaurant is not that far from the store," said Rosie.

Then Luisito saw the other two men who had also been following them.

"I don't like this," Luisito said, mumbling a Spanish proverb. "*Te conozco bacalao aunque vengas disfrasao*—I know you, codfish, even if you are in disguise. Those guys over there are Cuban and they are purposely following us."

"It's nothing, please, just a coincidence," Rosie said, smiling nervously. "I am Cuban as well. That doesn't mean anything."

"Yes, but the way they were following us and looking at us straight in the eyes is just like the intimidation they used in Cuba," Elena said.

"I am going to the bathroom," Sonia said, standing up and heading toward the back of the restaurant.

Rosie quickly excused herself and followed after her.

"Are you crazy, Sonia? You shouldn't be going anywhere by yourself. Those guys could be murderers on the loose stalking us!" Rosie said.

"Well, what happened to '*It's all a coincidence, this place is close to the store?*' " Sonia said.

"I don't want to scare them, because they just came from Cuba, but I am not taking any chances," Rosie whispered to Sonia, taking her daughter's hand and pulling her back toward the table.

"But, I need to go!" said Sonia.

"Hold it till we get home," said Rosie. "We are not going into that bathroom by ourselves."

"Shall we ask more people to join us?" said Sonia, smiling sarcastically, but Rosie ignored her comment and directed her right back to the table.

The men kept glancing toward their table as they spoke.

"Okay, that is it!" Sonia said. "I am going to go right up to him and ask him if he knows us."

The two Hispanic men threw their leftovers into the trash can by the exit and disappeared. A few minutes after the blond man did the same.

"No, he's leaving," Rosie said, grabbing Sonia by the arm. She looked playfully at Elena. "This girl could have never survived in communist Cuba."

# 15 QUINCE

The following Sunday morning Luisito joined his cousins in the kitchen early for breakfast. He was still amazed that all the appliances in the kitchen worked all the time and there were never any electricity shortages. The smell of peppers and onions lingered in the air. Rosie brought out of the oven a Spanish tortilla, a well-cooked potato omelet with onions and red peppers that looked a little like a cake.

The family hurried with their breakfast so they could get to Mass. Luisito's parents had given up going to Mass in Cuba because of fear, and now they found peace just by entering the church and listening to the beautiful music, looking at the religious art all around them, and praying with others. They especially wanted to thank God this Sunday for having received their working permits.

Miguel was now working as a secretary at a doctor's office during the day, and at night he was bagging groceries at a supermarket. He had two nights off from the grocery store, and he and Elena were attending English classes at a nearby high school. Once Miguel and Elena mastered English they could start studying to resume their former careers. Elena was working with Rosie at José's architecture firm. She helped with the filing and other office work. Rosie was the office manager.

It was hard work to balance so many things right now, but they were encouraged by all the other Cubans in the family who had done the same thing when they first came. They also had the advantage of living with family for as long as needed so they could save for their own place. Their new family seemed to enjoy having them at their home and didn't even want to speak about the day they were to move out.

Rosie put all the dirty dishes in the sink, cleaning her hands with a dish towel.

"Is everyone ready?" she asked.

"Yes, I will get my jacket," Luisito said. Although his cousins were still wearing short-sleeved shirts, the air was crisp—not what Luisito was used to.

Churches reminded Luisito of Abuela. He knew she would be going to church today. It was as if they were united in some strange way. The music coming from the choir caught his attention. The priest spoke, and then someone started reading. He wished he could understand the readings better. Then Tommy passed him a missalette, a book to follow along what the lector was reading. Luisito could read and understand English much better than he could speak it.

He watched attentively as the others sat, stood, and knelt. He loved the reading from the Gospel of Mark on how Jesus came to bring hope to all. He learned how Jesus healed, cured, and spread the word of God. This made Luisito very happy. It filled him with hope as well. Hope that he would make new friends, hope that his parents would have good jobs, and hope that Abuela would soon join them.

When the priest stepped to the ambo for the homily, Luisito tried to listen closely, but because it wasn't in Spanish he could only understand a few things. He heard the priest say that it was everyone's mission to live the Word of God and spread the Good News. Luisito wanted to read the Good News, but what in the world was that? Where could he find it? He would have to ask.

His mind had wandered a little when he heard a bell ring. He didn't know where it was coming from. He saw the priest lift a round piece of bread with great reverence and hold it high so everyone could see it. He did the same with a gold cup. Luisito was mesmerized. He saw the young priest's face and he imagined for a brief second that it was Jesus breaking the bread. The feeling made him shiver. He wondered what the others kneeling beside him felt. Some had their eyes closed and were absorbed in their conversation with God. Others looked at the altar and their lips moved as if they were holding a private conversation with someone. Luisito wondered how they had come to believe in God. He asked God to help him so he could soon understand and pray like those around him. Music began to play and people got up from the pews to receive this bread. This must be the Holy Bread that Abuela had spoken about. Luisito felt an urge to go when Rosie whispered in his ear.

"You have to learn more about the Holy Eucharist before you can receive it," she said.

Luisito sadly sat back down.

"But you may participate by staying in your seat and praying with the rest of the community," Rosie added.

Everyone sang one last hymn and then it was over. As they left Luisito noticed his mother was misty-eyed.

"I feel so good going to Mass," he heard her tell Rosie, "but at the same time so empty. I don't understand anything. I want to go to confession but there is no one here who speaks Spanish."

As they were walking toward the parking lot, Luisito saw a girl about his age. She had orange hair the color of a *calabasa*, or pumpkin, and the prettiest green eyes Luisito had ever seen.

"Hi, Tommy," she said, waving.

Luisito was glad she knew Tommy. This meant he would be meeting her.

"Hi, Sherry," Tommy said, and casually waved one hand. She looked at Luisito as she walked closer.

"This is my cousin Lewis," said Tommy.

"Hi, Lewis," she said, waving.

Luisito waved but was unable to say a word.

"Got to go," said Sherry. "Nice to meet you!"

Again, Luisito stared and waved.

"What happened to you?" Tommy asked when she had left. "First time I've seen you speechless. You like her or something?"

Luisito just nodded and stared.

"She is Sherry Jones," Tommy said. "She goes to my school and is on the soccer team. All the boys in my class like her, but they think she is a bit stuck up."

"Stuck to what?" asked Luisito.

"No, what I meant is that . . . she thinks she is all that," said Tommy.

"All what?" Luisito asked.

"She ignores most of the boys, so they think she isn't very nice, *comprendes?*" said Tommy.

"Yes, I get it," Luisito said. "She has the most beautiful red hair."

"Hey, speaking about soccer, do you want to try out with me this year?" Tommy said.

"Maybe," Luisito replied. "Her name is Che-rrrr-y?"

"No," Tommy said laughing. "Softer on the shhhh and don't roll your r's."

*Wow, I will have to practice that one*, Luisito thought. *What ever happened to all the Marias I used to know*, he wondered.

He wrote to Abuela that night and told her he had met the most beautiful girl with ginger hair and sparkling green eyes. He hoped he would hear back from Abuela soon. He knew he had to deliver the message she had whispered in his ear right before they left Cuba.

"Tell the Cuban priest at the Our Lady of Charity shrine in Miami this," she had said, "Exodus 32:1–35. It's a Bible verse. Memorize it. Also, tell him that his mother awaits him at the Italian Embassy."

When he had arrived in Maryland, Luisito had written Abuela's message down and hidden the piece of paper under his mattress. He was afraid that as time passed he would mix up the numbers or forget something. What could it all possibly mean?

# 16 DIECISÉIS

*Summer in the United States is wonderful,* Luisito thought. In Cuba there was always work to be done, but here Luisito and his cousins slept in, spent the day watching summer TV programs, played outside, and watched TV again until late at night.

During the day the adults were at work. Luisito felt so grown up. In Cuba, even when he stayed by himself he always had a neighbor come by to check up on him. Rosie did have two rules: no guests over while the adults were not home, and Sonia was not to drive them anywhere without permission. These were rules that his seventeen-year-old cousin didn't take very well, as the boys could tell by the disco music playing full blast in her bedroom.

"There she goes again!" Tommy said from the black vinyl reclining chair next to the TV. "Turn it down!" he shouted. "I can't hear *Gilligan's Island!*"

"Disco music is much better than that TV program," Sonia yelled as she lowered the music playing on her eight-track stereo. Then she came out to the living room, dancing and pointing alternately down to the ground and up to the sky. "It's *Saturday Night Fever*, baby!"

"Great, when she lowers the music the program ends," Tommy said. "I am so bored!"

Luisito couldn't understand how his cousin could be bored with all the games he owned, plus all the great television programs.

"I'm going to call my friends from the neighborhood," Tommy said.

"Didn't your mother say we couldn't have anyone over?" Luisito said.

"I am not going to let them inside the house. We can play basketball outside," he said.

"Okay, that sounds good," Luisito answered.

Tommy started calling his friends, and before long they were ringing the doorbell.

"This is my cousin from Cuba. His name is L-e-w-i-s. He will be starting school with us," Tommy said. "Lewis, these are my friends Bill, Steve, and Allen."

"Neat." "Cool." "Awesome," said each of the boys.

The name Lewis sounded strange to Luisito. I guess that's the way *Luis* is pronounced in English, he thought.

"Hi!" Luisito said to them.

"Where is Cuba, anyway?" one of the boys asked Luisito.

Luisito remained silent. Of course he understood what the boy was saying, but he was still self-conscious about speaking English.

"He doesn't speak English very well," Tommy answered.

"What does he speak, Cubanese?" asked Bill, the tallest one of the three.

"Spanish," said Tommy. "He came in a raft from Cuba."

"Cool!" said Allen, the boy with curly hair and dark skin.

"So, where did you say Cuba was?" Steve asked as he dribbled the basketball.

"It's an island about ninety miles from Florida in the Caribbean," Tommy said. "That's where my parents were born."

"That's cool. Can you play?" Bill said, tossing the basketball to Luisito. Luisito dribbled his way past all three. He jumped in the air and made a shot into the basket.

"He can play, all right!" Allen said.

"Hey, Lewis, I'm open," Steve called.

Luisito was not used to hearing his name pronounced this way so he didn't react at first.

"Lewis!" Steve continued to shout. Luisito passed him the ball, and he made the shot.

They continued to play for the next thirty minutes, Steve and Luisito against Tommy and Bill. Allen was taking a break drinking soda and acting like the referee when he noticed something strange at the opposite end of the block.

"What are you looking at?" Steve asked, glancing at a white Ford Granada parked by one of the houses.

"Mike's dad doesn't own a Ford, does he?" Allen said, pointing.

"Where is Mike, anyway?" Steve asked.

"He's away for summer camp," Tommy said. "You know, in New York, where he goes every year."

"Whatever, let's keep playing," Bill said, throwing the ball to Luisito.

"Wait, guys," Allen said. "I think there is a man inside the car. I just saw a head with a baseball cap pop up from the back seat and take a picture of us!"

"That's crazy!" Tommy said. "I don't see anyone. Let's go with our bikes and check it out!"

Tommy, Allen, and Steve jumped on their bikes and headed toward the car.

All of a sudden someone sprang up in the front seat. The car swerved around, driving over the curb as it sped away.

"Wow, did you see that?" Tommy said.

"Weird!" Bill exclaimed.

"We scared him off!" Allen said.

Luisito walked slowly behind because he didn't have a bike.

"I'm actually hungry," he said nervously. "Let's have lunch."

"Yeah, that is a good idea," Tommy said. They all went back to Tommy's front porch.

"Why do you think they were taking a picture of us?" Bill said.

"Some weirdo, probably," Allen said.

"Well, I'm getting hungry too. I'm heading home," Bill said. "Hey, Lewis, nice meeting you!"

"It's Luis," Luisito said. It sounded like *loo-EES*, but his new friends had a hard time picking up on the pronunciation.

That night during dinner, Tommy and Luisito were eager to tell the story of the strange men hiding in the car. Elena and Miguel looked at them with concern.

"And we scared them off!" Tommy said with a mouth full of *picadillo*.

"You should not have chased them. They could have hurt you," José said.

"They could be robbers spying on empty homes!" Rosie said. "I don't think it is safe for you boys to play outside while we are not home."

"Oh, Mom," Tommy said. "I've always played outside. I've gone as far as the back woods and nothing has ever happened to me."

"Well, we haven't seen burglars in our neighborhood before," she said.

"You should ask the neighbors if they have seen those cars here before," José said, looking at Rosie.

"The other day someone followed us in the store and to a fast-food restaurant," Rosie said. "This neighborhood seems to be changing. Some very strange things are happening."

"Mom, there is nothing wrong with the neighborhood," Sonia said. "It was obvious, the creepy guy was after me."

"Yeah, you are just his type," Tommy said laughing. "Creepy!"

"Stop it, you two," Rosie said.

Tommy and Sonia were smiling at each other, but the adults were quite serious. Elena and Miguel, especially, didn't take the news of someone following the family very lightly.

Luisito had caught half of the car's license plate and he would be on the lookout for the other half. He had an eerie feeling he would be seeing that car again.

# 17 DIECISIETE

The two Hispanic-looking men in the car sped away. Antonio, who had slick greased hair and bad acne, was driving. Jorge had longer hair in a ponytail and was wearing a Yankees baseball cap and sunglasses. They had taken the pictures they needed, and now they couldn't wait to develop them in their makeshift dark-room.

"The boy looks like he has lived here all his life," said Antonio.

"Who wouldn't adjust easily to this good life?" Jorge said, laughing.

"Has the thought of defecting ever crossed your mind?" Antonio asked bluntly.

It actually had crossed Jorge's mind many times but he wasn't about to tell Antonio that. Even though he had worked with Antonio for years, he didn't trust him. He didn't trust anyone. Anyone in Cuba could rat on anyone else to rise in the government. The Communist Party rewarded and encouraged this type of behavior. Jorge himself had gotten this great job infiltrating the United States by spying on fellow Cubans and turning them in. It was just his way of surviving and providing for his family, he told himself. He would defect in a minute except that it was too complicated to get his whole family out.

"Never!" Jorge said, smiling. "The Cuban government gives us all we need. Imagine if I came to this country and I had to start bagging groceries or mopping restaurant floors."

"I am with you on that," Antonio said after a long pause. "The Cuban government is good to us and our families. This assignment is the best job in the world!"

They parked their car at the downtown apartment they had rented in Baltimore.

"What do you think about the American who is following them?" Jorge asked. "FBI or CIA?"

"Who cares?" Antonio shot back quickly. "We got the pictures. That is what the people back home needed. We haven't committed any crimes. They can't do anything to us."

"Do you think they will be on our trail?"

"We will clean up this apartment and move on to our place in Miami soon. We can change our appearance a bit," Antonio said. "How would I look as a blond?"

"Pretty ugly!" Jorge said, laughing. Yet he was sure this assignment would not be an easy one. It was one of those feelings.

# 18 DIECIOCHO

The weekend before school started Luisito packed all his new supplies and laid out his clothes for Monday.

"Boy, you are ahead of the game!" Tommy said when he stepped into their room. He still had everything scattered in his closet.

Sunday night Luisito went to bed early. He had an uneasy feeling about his first day of school. He had spent the previous night asking Tommy questions about high school.

Back in Cuba, Luisito knew everyone from school because they all lived in the same neighborhood. At least, he thought, his cousins would be there and the boys from his new neighborhood. That wasn't so bad. He realized he knew a few people already. As Tommy had pointed out, he was better off than most people who move into a new town.

It seemed that he had only been asleep a few minutes when his alarm rang. He jumped quickly out of bed and dressed in his alligator shirt, jeans, and new sneakers. He went straight to the bathroom to wash his face and gel his hair as the barber had taught him.

He then ran downstairs, where his parents were already eating breakfast.

"*¡El primero día de colegio!*" his mom said excitedly, referring to the first day of school.

"Yes, we start school today. Bummer," Tommy said as he came into the kitchen still in his pajamas. "I love to sleep in during the summer."

"He is such a *dormilón*," José said, patting his son in the back.

"Education is important," Luisito's father said. "In this country, you have the opportunity to be whatever you want and be successful."

Luisito placed his new book bag by the door. He ate his breakfast carefully so as not to get dirty.

"*¿No quieres más?*" Rosie asked, like always.

"No, thanks. I don't want anything else to eat. I am full," Luisito said, patting his stomach.

Sonia came rushing down the stairs. She was wearing a light blue headband that matched her blouse and a wide belt with a big, shiny silver buckle in front. She actually looked very pretty, Luisito thought.

"If you need to you can always take that belt off and use it for security measures," her dad joked.

"Funny, Dad!" she said, pouring orange juice in her glass. "It's the fashion."

Luisito went to the bathroom to take one more look in the mirror. He wanted to pinch himself. Was this really him? He looked so different—he *felt* so different.

"Let's go!" he heard Sonia yell.

"Wait, honey, let me take a picture of you all!" Rosie said.

The three of them posed for the picture.

"Isn't this great!" Luisito said to Tommy. He never even owned a camera in Cuba. Tommy gave him a strange look.

"Come on, Mom, take the picture so we can go," Tommy pleaded.

"Oh, pleeeease, Mom, hurry," Sonia said. "She does this every year," she told Luisito, rolling her eyes.

"She does? That's great!" Luisito said. His cousins look at him, surprised. "What? I love pictures!"

When they arrived at school, there were kids hanging around the entrance of the school building speaking with one another, and others were walking in clusters toward the door. Rosie parked the car.

"Shall I walk you to your classrooms?" she asked

"Noooo!" Sonia and Tommy answered as if on cue.

"I would rather die," Sonia said.

*"¡Qué exagerada!"* Rosie said. "Drama queen!"

"Mom, I know where to go. I will take Luisitio," Tommy said.

"Sure?" said Rosie.

*"No problema,"* said Tommy.

"Okay, kids, off to school. Have a great day," Rosie said.

Luisito walked with Tommy through big aluminum doors that opened to a wide hallway full of students walking in different directions. Luisito looked around the hallway at the students' clothes and book bags. He had never paid much attention to these things in Cuba.

"We always start the day coming to this class," Tommy explained to Luisito. "This is home room, you know, like your main *casa*."

They sat down and were given a copy of their schedules and other forms to take home to fill out. The teacher, a young woman with short blond hair and freckles, welcomed everyone to their freshman year and promised them an exciting school year.

"Did you hear that? We are going to have an exciting year," Luisito said to Tommy.

"They always say that," Tommy shrugged.

A bell rang and they had to change classes. Luisito didn't have to change classes as many times back in Cuba; there, the teachers came to his classroom while the students stayed in their seats. He liked this much better! Tommy looked at Luisito's schedule, and, as he had suspected, it was the same as his, except during English grammar. Luisito was sent to ESOL class, English for Speakers of Other Languages, on the second floor.

In math class, the teacher, Mrs. Kelly, asked everyone what they did during the summer. A familiar voice yelled from the back of the class.

"Lewis came rafting from Cuba!" the boy said. When Luisito turned around, he saw Allen smiling at him.

"Oh, how interesting," Mrs. Kelly said. "Can you tell us more about it?"

"My English is not so good," Luisito said.

"Don't worry. Come to the front of the class and practice," she said.

Luisito stood up slowly, wiping his sweaty hands on his new jeans. His heart was beating fast. He looked down at his new shoes and then up into the faces of his new classmates.

"I escaped from Cuba at night," Luisito started, "with my mother and father. We came in a raft and the sea was full of waves but the Coast Guard finally rescued us. We now live with my cousin Tommy."

Luisito heard giggles from some girls sitting on the left side of the classroom. He wondered why they found this funny.

"That was excellent, Lewis," Mrs. Kelly said as the bell rang. As he gathered his papers, Tommy motioned to him.

"Hey, Luisito," Tommy whispered. "Here in school I go by Thomas, just so you know."

"And I now go by Lewis," Luisito said, smiling, "just so you know."

"I hear ya," Tommy said, laughing. They walked out of the classroom together.

# 19 DIECINUEVE

The next day Luisito got to school earlier than usual. The bell rang at school and Luisito walked toward his first period class. He noticed the kids he passed in the hallway were wearing sweaters. Luisito, used to the warm breezes of the Caribbean, was already freezing. Wearing his blue jacket, he walked quickly toward Room 102: history class with Mr. Xavier Alvarez. History was Luisito's favorite subject, and he remembered his teacher in Cuba once spoke about the American Revolution. Of course, he didn't exactly know what was true or not. According to Abuela, his teachers were known for bending the truth about history.

"How many students are new this year?" Mr. Alvarez asked.

Three students, including Luisito, raised their hands.

"Well, we have something in common. I'm new to this school too," Mr. Alvarez said, smiling.

"We are going to start our semester learning about Latin America and the Caribbean. Is anyone in this class from those places?"

A girl from Honduras, a boy from Jamaica, and Luisito each stood up and told where they were from.

"I am originally from Mexico, but I came here to study and then stayed," Mr. Alvarez said. "The United States is composed of immigrants from different parts of the world."

He wrote down where the three students were from and said he would start with those countries.

"We can start with Cuba since it is the closest country to the United States," he said.

"Where did you live, Lewis?" Mr. Alvarez asked.

"In Havana," Luisito responded.

"And your dad, what did he do for a living?" Mr. Alvarez said.

"He is a medical doctor," Luisito answered.

"Then your father must come and talk to our class one day," Mr. Alvarez said, just as the bell rang.

Luisito couldn't wait to tell his father that he had been invited to speak in his class.

"Do you think your father is going to want to speak to the class?" Tommy whispered.

"He won't have much to say," said Luisito. "He worked in a neighborhood hospital. It's only the hospitals where the tourists go that have everything."

"By the way, did you sign up for soccer?" Tommy asked, handing him two forms.

Right after dinner that night, Luisito gave the forms that he had filled out to his mother so she could sign them.

"Who's this *Lewis*?" asked Elena, looking at the form.

"That's his American name," said Tommy, who was sitting at the dinner table with them.

"Look at him. Before we know it he will forget all his Spanish!" Rosie said as she cut herself a piece of apple pie.

"He'd better not," Miguel smiled at them. "Luis Alberto Miguel Angel Ramirez Jemot!"

# 20 VEINTE

"Luisito!" Sonia yelled, running in the house. "Miguel, Elena, everyone come here!" Sonia waved a letter in the air. "It's from your grandmother! A letter from Cuba!"

Everyone gathered to open the envelope. Inside there was a letter for Luisito's parents and another for Luisito. Elena and Miguel sat down to read their letter. Luisito ran to his bedroom to read his.

*Querido Luisito,*

*I am so glad you are having a great time with all our family! How is school?*

*When I walked past the park the other day I saw your friends Mayito, Roberto, and Carmen. They all asked about you. I told them you went to the United States.*

*I miss you terribly but I am full of joy every time I receive a letter from you and your parents.*

*Despite my arthritis, I am doing just fine. A neighbor brought me a mango the other day. I remembered how much you loved them.*

*I love you with all my heart!*

*Abuela*

*P.S. Don't forget . . . that I love you very much!*

Luisito read the letter several times to look for hidden clues. In Cuba, the government often monitored letters and phone calls. Therefore, people wrote in clues. Obviously, when Abuela said not to forget she was referring to the secret mission. He held the letter tight to his heart. How he missed Abuela and his friends! If only they could all come here. Then he would be completely happy.

"Luisito, are you all right?" Elena called, knocking gently on his door.

Luisito wiped tears from his face. "Sure, coming," he said.

Luisito and his parents sat down and compared their letters. Abuela wasn't very explicit in either one.

That night Luisito remembered that Abuela was probably praying right at that moment. Rosie said that those who spent time speaking to God and developing a friendship with him would have their prayers answered. She said this was possible if they asked God sincerely and if God deemed that what they were asking was indeed the best for them. He wished he had a relationship with

God just like Abuela did. Maybe then God would hear his prayers faster! Luisito looked at Tommy, who was reading a book in his bed.

"Hey, Tommy," Luisito said. "Tell me more about God."

Tommy put his book down.

"About God?" he said, surprised.

"Yes!" Luisito said very seriously.

"Okay," Tommy said scratching his head. "Well, he is our Father. He loves us and forgives us, and he hears our prayers."

"I don't know how to pray by myself," Luisito said.

"Well, you just talk to him like you would to a friend," Tommy said. "You've never done that before?"

"Not really," Luisito said. "In Cuba, I listened to Abuela's prayers at night and kind of followed along. I did try praying by myself during my trip on the ocean."

"Well, you must have done a good job because he heard you. You made it," Tommy said, smiling.

Luisito hadn't really thought about that. God did hear him. The thought gave him peace.

"I can't wait to go to Miami," Luisito said, changing the subject.

"I love Miami," Tommy said. "I can't wait to see my grandmother. She makes me all my favorite desserts. I also love the beach!"

Luisito didn't know if he could trust his cousin with his big secret. Abuela had told him not to tell anyone, but could she have meant not to tell the adults? His teenage cousins could do no harm. They knew very little about politics or anything like that. Luisito wanted to tell Tommy his secret because it felt like *una papa caliente*, a steaming hot potato, in his hands, but he decided to wait a little longer.

"Do you have a Bible?" Luisito said.

"Yeah, under my bed," Tommy said.

"Why do you keep it there?" Luisito said.

"That's where I keep all my important stuff," Tommy answered. "Here," he said, handing the book to Luisito.

Luisito leafed through the many pages with no idea of where to start.

"Do you know how to use it?" Tommy asked.

"Not really," he said.

"What do you want to read?" Tommy asked.

"Exodus 32:1–35," Luisito answered very matter-of-factly.

"Hold it," Tommy said. "You have never opened a Bible and you want to read precisely that Bible verse?"

"I saw a man holding it on a poster on the street," Luisito lied. *What a save*, he thought. He actually had seen a homeless man with a sign when he went to the mall, but it said something about asking for food.

"Let's find out," Tommy said, smiling and sitting cross-legged on his bed with the Bible on his lap.

"When Moses delayed coming down from the mountain, the people gathered around Aaron and said to him, 'Come, make us a god who will be our leader,'" Tommy read from the Bible at a fast pace.

"Wait!" Luisito interrupted. "You read it and then tell me what it's about because I don't understand anything you're saying."

"I saw this in the movie *The Ten Commandments*," Tommy said. "It's about the golden calf."

"Golden calf?" Luisito said, shrugging his shoulders. "Makes no sense to me."

"Wait, let me read the whole thing," Tommy said, quickly skimming the passage.

"Okay, the Exodus is when God delivered the Israelites from Egyptian rule. He did this by parting the seas," Tommy said. "The Israelites were slaves. Understand?"

"Okay," Luisito said.

"This part of the book of Exodus talks about Moses going to the mountain for prayer with God. While he is gone the Israelites forget about the Ten Commandments and build themselves a golden calf. They worshiped the calf and did all sorts of sinful things and . . ."

"I don't get it," Luisito interrupted. He was trying to make sense of why his grandmother needed him to tell this to a priest in Miami. Wouldn't he know this? Wouldn't he have read the Bible many times already? So far, Exodus dealt with a massive fleeing of the Egyptians through the sea and a golden icon. None of it made much sense to Luisito.

Then there was the other part of the message: "Your mother is waiting for you in Italy." What did this Bible verse have to do with the Cuban priest's mother being in Italy? Unless she was coming to Miami and bringing a precious Bible with her? No, that didn't make sense because the message referred to Exodus, not to the whole Bible. Maybe his mother was escaping by sea from Cuba and waiting for him in Italy?

"Well, I am reading more," Tommy said, running his index finger down the page. "They got busted! When Moses came back he and God were very upset at the way these people had behaved. They totally forgot what God had done for them."

"It doesn't make sense," Luisito repeated to himself.

"What doesn't make sense?" Tommy asked.

"Oh . . . why the man would be holding a poster with this information," Luisito lied again. Could he trust his cousin to keep the secret? He wondered again why Abuela would want to keep this a secret when she had always told him to go to an adult in time of need. Maybe she was afraid that his parents would not want him to get involved.

"You know, Tommy . . ." Luisito was about to tell him when they were interrupted.

"To sleep, everyone!" José said, turning off the lights.

"We are in high school already, Papi!" Tommy said.

"No, excuses!" José replied. "*El que duerme primero duerme mejor*—the one who sleeps first sleeps best!"

"Huh?" Tommy said quizzically. Luisito looked at him and they started laughing.

# 21 VEINTIUNO

This morning the school hallway smelled of fresh lemon scent. Luisito took a deep, breath. He knew that in a few hours, with the change of class, the air would be permeated with a mixture of girls' perfume, jockey sweat, and chalk dust. As the bell rang, Luisito swiftly passed the other students rushing to their next class period. He heard some boys mention that the list of those who had made the soccer team was posted outside the physical education classroom.

Luisito looked at the glass-covered bulletin board to see if he had made it, but he didn't see his name. Then he saw Tommy's and Sherry's. The coaches had posted the lists for the boys' and the girls' team side by side.

"Hey, Lewis," said Paul, a friend of Sonia's. "How come your name is not on the list? I thought all Hispanics were good at soccer. It's in your blood."

A few other boys laughed and walked away.

"Remember me? I'm Paul," he said, shaking Luisito's hand. "Why don't you try out for basketball? You look tall enough." He handed Luisito a flyer with all the information.

"Thanks, I will," Luisito said.

The next morning, Luisito headed off for basketball tryouts. He didn't know why he was doing this or what he was proving, but he wanted to join something.

He heard that the coach usually picked most of the older boys for the team, so his chances were minimal. He had never played on the school team in Cuba, but he had played at the park all the time with his friends.

There were about twenty boys at the tryouts. The coach had them dribble the ball from one side of the court to the other. They did layups and free throws. The coach had them sprint from one side of the court to the other to measure their speed. Finally, he separated the players in groups and had them scrimmage.

The coach, a big man who looked more like a football player than a basketball coach, gathered them to stretch after tryouts were over. He mentioned that it would be tough to pick the right team because everyone this year was so impressive. He would have to think about this thoroughly and by the end of the week he would post the list. The first practice was the next Monday, and the first game of the season was in two weeks.

"We had a good season last year, and we hope this year we can be undefeated! " Coach Jerry said.

"Yeah!" the boys cheered in unison.

Then Luisito grabbed his backpack and towel, and he headed toward the school office. He had to call Sonia to see if she could pick him up. He opened the glass office door and, when he looked toward the waiting area, there was Sherry, reading a book. She looked up and smiled.

"Hi, Sherry," Luisito said. "What are you doing here?"

"We had a soccer meeting and now I am waiting for my mother," she said. "I have dance class today."

"I saw your name on the soccer list," Luisito said, sitting beside her. "Congratulations on making the team."

"Thank you!" Sherry responded with a big smile. "Did you try out for basketball today?

"Yes, it was tough." he said. "Listen, I've tried calling you a couple times but you are never home after school."

"Oh," she said, sounding surprised, "I didn't know you had called. I have something almost every day after school. Here, give me your number," she handed him a piece of paper.

Luisito went blank. He couldn't remember Tommy's phone number. He hardly used it. Then he remembered he had written it on something in his wallet. He felt like a clown taking it out of his wallet and copying it down for her. He gave Sherry the paper, which she folded and put in her purse.

At that moment, Sherry's mom walked into the school office. Luisito had seen her a couple of times from a distance at Mass and had spoken to her over the phone, but he had never been introduced to her. Mrs. Jones was a very elegant woman, tall and slender, with dark red hair.

"Let's go, sweetie, I'm in a hurry," she said without noticing Luisito.

"Mom, this is Lewis," Sherry said, gesturing toward Luisito. "He's the Cuban boy I told you about."

"Is this Thomas's cousin? The one who arrived from Cuba?" she said.

"Yes, I am," Luisito responded. "How are you?"

"Fine, thank you," she said as they shook hands. "By the way, does your father do garden work? We are starting a landscaping project."

"No, he is isn't good with plants," Luisito said.

"How about construction?" she asked.

Luisito shook his head.

"Well, what does he do?" she asked, puzzled.

"He is a medical doctor," Luisito said.

"A doctor! I would have never thought of that," she said. "I was sure I saw him bagging groceries the other day at the supermarket."

"Yes, that's him. It's his part-time job. He works in a doctor's office in the morning. He is also taking more English classes and planning on getting his . . . ugh . . . *licencia?*" Luisito answered.

"You mean license?" Sherry offered.

Luisito nodded and smiled.

"Well, good for him!" Mrs. Jones said. "Say hi to Rosie for us."

Sherry waved, and she and Mrs. Jones walked out the door as Luisito held it open for them. He replayed their conversation in his head. He hoped he had spoken English correctly. Then he remembered he needed to call Sonia to pick him up. He asked permission to use the phone.

At that moment, Mr. Alvarez walked in the door and looked in his direction.

"Hey, *Cubanito!*" he said, patting him in the back. "Tomorrow we will be talking about the weather and vegetation of Cuba."

"Great!" Luisito said. He walked out into the hallway and toward the main door to wait for Sonia. He saw a girl with long, curly, brown hair updating the bulletin board. She was just putting up a flyer when all the rest slipped out of her hands and fell across the hallway. Luisito ran to help her.

"Thank you," she said, smiling at Luisito. "Aren't you the Cuban refugee?"

"I guess so," Luisito said, not liking the tone of the word refugee.

"I am Cristina," she said swinging her ponytail. "My family is from El Salvador. Why don't you join the Spanish Club? We meet every Tuesday after school."

"I am trying out for basketball," he said. "Thanks, anyway."

"Is Sherry your girlfriend?" Cristina asked.

"We are friends," Luisito said.

"Is this the first time you have met her mother?" she asked.

"Yes," he said.

"I see . . . well, according to my mother, Mrs. Jones doesn't like Hispanics too much," Cristina whispered to him.

"You mean . . . *¿que nos mastica pero no nos traga?*" Luisito said, not liking where the conversation was heading. The Spanish saying "she can chew us but not swallow us" meant she had a subtle prejudice against foreigners.

"That's what my mother says," Cristina said. "But you didn't hear it from me."

Luisito waved good-bye to her and left quickly. He wasn't sure if what this girl had said about Mrs. Jones was true, but she had looked at him rather strangely. When Luisito arrived home, he could hear his family all cheering at the TV set. He wondered what sport they were watching.

*"Ese Reagan se la comió!"* Miguel said.

"What did Ronald Reagan eat?" Tommy asked.

"That is an expression," Rosie said laughing. "It means he is incredible!"

"What an inspiring speech!" Elena said. "I hope he becomes president."

Luisito went to the kitchen to see what was for dinner today. It was his mother's turn to cook, and she was following a recipe she had found in Rosie's cookbook. Rosie was beside her helping to chop up green peppers and other vegetables for the *sofrito*, or marinade.

"It's *fricassee de pollo* tonight," Elena said proudly.

"Good, I like chicken," Luisito said.

"How was your day?" Elena asked.

"It was good. I met Sherry's mother," he said.

"Well, you don't sound too happy about that," Rosie said.

Luisito explained what his classmate had told him about Mrs. Jones.

"Who told you that?" Tommy asked as he walked into the kitchen.

"Just someone from school," Luisito said.

"It may or may not be true," Rosie said, pausing in her work. "Mrs. Jones has always been very nice to me, but I've never dealt with her socially."

"Don't believe everything you hear, son," Elena said. "You have to know people and make your own judgments."

Luisito poured himself a cup of milk and drank it while food was being prepared. His thoughts then turned to Sherry and her family. Would they not like him because he was from a different country?

# 22 VEINTIDÓS

That Friday, Luisito rushed to the gym to see the list of who had made the basketball team. There was a big crowd so he couldn't see the list. Some of the guys left quietly; others were high-fiving and congratulating each other. Luisito waited patiently for his turn to see the list.

"Hey, Lewis!" Paul called to him. "You made the team, man."

Luisito felt a great relief.

"You too?" Luisito asked. He already knew the answer because Paul was one of the best players at the tryouts.

"Yep, can't wait to start winning!" Paul said, very excited.

Finally, Luisito had joined a school team. He would have his first practice next week and soon, maybe, new friends. He desperately wanted to fit in.

He looked down the hall and saw Sherry coming with books in hand to check the list. Maybe she was looking for his name, Luisito hoped.

"I made it!" Luisito said as she approached.

"That's great!" she exclaimed. "I knew you would."

"Hey, some of us are going to the movies tomorrow. Want to come?" Luisito said.

"I'd love to!" Sherry said. "Maybe after the movie we can have sodas at that shop where everyone goes."

"Great!" Luisito said. "I will call you for your address. Wait. Why don't you just give it to me now?"

Sherry gave him her address. Luisito waved and walked down the hall feeling a little taller.

✦ ✦ ✦

All during school the next day, Luisito could not stop thinking about going to the movies with Sherry.

Luisito went through dinner in a daze. He showered, ate, and dressed in a polo shirt that he borrowed from Tommy and his own blue jeans and sneakers.

When they got to Sherry's house, Sonia stayed in the car and Luisito rang the doorbell. Sherry opened the door. She was wearing a light green dress and her hair was pulled up in a ponytail with a white ribbon. The green picked up the color of her eyes.

"For you," Luisito said, giving her a small bouquet of flowers he had just picked up at the grocery store.

"That is so sweet!" Sherry said, smelling the flowers. "Are we ready to go?"

"I think I should speak to your mother first," he said.

"Oh, okay," she said turning around. "Mom," she yelled inside.

"Yes?" Mrs. Jones stepped to the door in an apron.

"Mrs. Jones," Luisito said. "How are you?"

"Fine, thank you," Mrs. Jones said, a bit puzzled.

"A group of us are going to the movies and later we will have a snack. I will be bringing Sherry back at about nine."

"Good. Although it's not a school night, I like her to be back early," Mrs. Jones said.

"Oh, Mom," Sherry said, turning to hand her the flowers Luisito had given to her. "Can you put these in water? Lewis gave them to me."

Mrs. Jones smelled the flowers and for the first time Luisito saw Mrs. Jones smile.

"How lovely," she said and waved to Sonia in the car. "Have fun now!"

At the movies, Luisito bought a bucket of popcorn and two sodas. They decided to see a comedy that had just been released. When the movie was over, they all went to the soda shop at the corner of the plaza. Everyone sat down in a booth: Tommy, Allen, a girl named Emily, her next-door neighbor Tracy, and Sonia, who was going to drive them home. There was no room for Luisito and Sherry, so they sat at another table not too far away.

"I am so full from all the popcorn and soda," Sherry said. "Why don't we split a cheesecake?"

"That's good," Luisito said.

"Can we please have one cheesecake to share?" Sherry told the waiter, who nodded and hurried to the kitchen.

He returned with a slice of cheesecake and two forks.

"Mmm, this is good," Luisito said. "I never had cheesecake in Cuba."

Luisito told Sherry the stories his grandmother used to tell him about Cuba and how different it was before he was born.

"Tell me about your escape again," Sherry said.

Luisito recounted his journey, the storm, the broken motor, and his long hours of rowing. He told her how glad he was to be in this country but how he missed his grandmother and the friends he left behind.

"Oh, Lewis," she said, "you know what I like the most about you? That you don't take anything for granted. You enjoy everything, even cheesecake!"

"You know what I like the most about you?" Luisito said. "When I see you close your eyes to pray at church. I have never seen anyone my own age pray that way."

Sherry told Luisito how prayer had helped her cope with her parents' divorce and how last year her parents had gotten back together.

"It was painful," Sherry said. "Prayer didn't make the pain go away, but it helped me to know that God was with me."

"I understand," Luisito said. "I am glad your parents are back together. You know if you ever need someone to talk to, I'm here."

"Thank you," she said, smiling.

# 23 VEINTITRÉS

On Monday, Luisito hurried to the gym for basketball practice. The coach and his assistants had the students do layups, sprinting, and other drills. He also split them into teams and had them play a short game so they could practice their offense and defense.

Coach Jerry explained the strength and weaknesses of each one on the team and how they needed to complement one another if they wanted to win this season.

"Lewis, you have speed and you make good shots. Just work on your layups. Danny, don't stop when you are dribbling. You will get called for a double dribble. Eric, bend those knees when you are going to take that free throw . . ." Coach Jerry continued.

That week, Luisito practiced hard every day with the team at school. When he got home right before dinner he practiced some more with the hoop outside the house. He paid attention to all the plays Coach Jerry drew in his notebook. He understood the plays well since they were drawn.

His first game was on Friday. The team won but he hadn't played. He sat on the bench the whole game. This continued game after game. Luisito stopped telling his parents to come to the games because he hardly ever got called to play. Sherry came anyway, but it was embarrassing that he sat on the bench most of the time. He didn't want to seem upset, so every game he smiled and cheered for his team, giving them high fives when they finished a quarter and listening attentively to all the plays. Paul told him that Coach Jerry rarely put in new players when the score was close, but if they were ever winning by a large margin, Luisito would definitely get a chance to play.

During the playoffs Eric had broken his ankle and was in a cast, so Paul was their point guard for this game. The score was 20–18 in their favor in the first quarter. In the second quarter the score got closer and closer.

They were now in the fourth quarter. The score was 40–38 and the other team was winning. Paul passed the ball to Ron, who tried to shoot, but his attempt was blocked by the other team. They tried the play again, and Paul was double-teamed before he could pass the ball. As he tried to break free he fell, twisting his ankle. Coach Jerry helped him to the bench while the crowd applauded.

The coach asked for a timeout. The team huddled, and Coach Jerry motioned to Luisito. "Come over here, Lewis," he said. "You're going in."

Luisito jumped up and ran over.

"Ron, you take over as point guard. Pass the ball to Lewis. Lewis, you get close and make that shot. We are not asking you to make a three pointer. Just help us tie the game," Coach Jerry explained.

The whistle blew and Luisito ran onto the court. The other team grabbed the ball and made their way down the court. Luisito found himself right beside the player with the ball. He stuck his hand out and grabbed the ball while the other player was dribbling. He sped all the way to the other end of the court. He glanced around and didn't see anyone near him. He shot—and made it! All his team players rushed to high-five him. Now they were tied. After a timeout, the game started again, and the other team had the ball. They were running fast when Ron, who was in midcourt, swiftly took the ball from his opponent and threw it, making the shot seconds before the horn sounded. The Lions won by two points! They were going to the championship game!

Coach Jerry congratulated each one of them for their performance.

"Lewis, you were great! Good job. You used your instincts and that's what counts. You got us in the game again," Coach Jerry said, smiling.

Sonia and Rosie came down the bleachers and hugged Luisito. They pointed to the movie camera. They had everything on film to show Luisito's parents, who were at night class, studying English.

As they were leaving, Luisito saw the local sports reporter who came to every game. He took notes on the
games and even took pictures of the team. But that night,
Luisito saw him toss his notebook in the trash can as he
left. *This man is no local sports reporter*, Luisito thought. *He
is watching someone.* The thought frightened him.

# 24 VEINTICUATRO

Luisito was very excited about the championship game coming up, but he was even more concerned about getting to Miami.

"Are we going to Miami for Christmas?" Luisito asked one night at dinner.

"I am not sure if your father can get time off from work," José said.

"That is true, Luisito," his dad said.

"I really want to go" Luisito said.

"Don't worry. If we can't go now we will go for spring vacation," Rosie said.

Luisito quietly finished his dinner, pondering how to get to Florida.

That night he remembered that Abuela always prayed when she needed to make a decision. He could try that as well. He closed his eyes and found himself praying to Our Lady of Charity and asking her to guide him to her shrine somehow. He opened his eyes and waited. He wondered how she would guide him. Would a limo suddenly be waiting at his door? Would God phone him? The thought made Luisito smile, but in all seriousness he didn't know how our Lady could help him. For a minute the whole prayer thing seemed absurd, but all he could do was trust and hope that things would turn out right, just as Abuela trusted.

He was getting sleepy. His body ached from the grueling basketball practices. As he lay there he suddenly realized that he couldn't do this on his own. He needed to trust someone with his secret.

"Tommy, are you awake?" Luisito asked.

Tommy rolled over. "What is it?" he said sleepily.

"Do you think Sonia could drive us to Miami?" asked Luisito.

"You've got to be kidding," he said.

"Why not?" Luisito said.

"Number one, Mom would kill her," said Tommy, now wide awake. "Number two," he said, pausing. "Number two doesn't actually matter because, as I said before, Mom would kill her."

"It's really important," Luisito started explaining in a whisper. "Before I left Cuba Abuela whispered something in my ear."

Tommy was sitting up in bed with his eyes wide open. "What did she say?" he asked.

"She told me it was very important to tell a particular Cuban priest in Miami these two things," he said, pausing.

"Well?" Tommy wanted to know.

"First, she said to tell him Exodus 32:1–35, and then she said to let him know that his mother was waiting for him in Italy," Luisito said, feeling a sudden relief to share that with someone.

"Creepy!" Tommy said.

"Why do you say that?" Luisito said.

"Well, that was the same Bible verse on the sign of the man you saw on the street," Tommy said.

"No, no," Luisito said. "I made that up. Sorry. I just wanted you to read that Bible verse to me. I wasn't ready to tell you the secret just then."

"Why?" Tommy said. "What's the big mystery? Tell my folks and then they would make sure to take us to Miami quickly."

"That would be easy, but Abuela also said not to tell anyone," Luisito said. "I had to tell you because there is no way I can get to Miami without your help."

"Why would she say not to tell anyone?" Tommy said.

At that moment, Sonia knocked on the door, then opened it without waiting for a response.

"Hey, Tommy," she said, "did you leave the phone off the hook?"

"Oops, sorry," he said, looking toward the phone stand in his room.

"Great!" Sonia was visibly upset. "I'm sure he called me and couldn't get through!"

"Who's he?" said Luisito to Tommy.

"Beats me," he answered and shrugged.

"I heard that!" said Sonia as she stomped away.

"Wait!" Luisito yelled. "We need to talk to you."

"I don't think that is a good idea," Tommy said.

"Well, it's the only idea I have right now," Luisito said.

"What mess did you guys get into?" Sonia asked, walking back into the room.

Luisito told her about the secret and how she couldn't tell anyone.

"Of course, you can count on me!" she said, smiling. "This is the most exciting thing that has happened to me since William asked me to go to junior prom with him!"

"I say we do like in the movies and set out on an adventure, just the three of us," said Tommy, getting very excited.

"Yes, brilliant idea. We can get into all sorts of trouble . . . *or* we could tell Mom and get the job done quickly," Sonia said.

"I hate when she is all practical," Tommy said, making a face.

"Well, what if she tells my parents and they don't want me to get involved and I can't carry out Abuela's plan?" Luisito said.

"We'll tell her to keep it a secret," Sonia replied. "She won't tell anyone because we are 'doing it for Cuba.'" Sonia smiled. "You know how she always wants us to feel proud of our heritage."

"She's got a point," Tommy said, looking at Luisito.

"Okay. I will tell her tomorrow after dinner," Luisito said.

"Tell her now," Sonia said. "Your parents are in their room and she is watching a movie with Dad."

"I wanted to tell her alone," Luisito said.

"Oh, Dad fell asleep beside her," Sonia said. "Mom had to put up the volume because of his snoring. Go, go now!"

Luisito got up from his bed to go talk to Rosie. A minute ago he had felt relief in sharing his secret with his cousins, but now he was afraid. Two people knew and he had to tell a third.

Luisito slowly tiptoed down the stairs. How would he tell her? What if she said no and told his parents? Is this what Abuela would want him to do?

# 25 VEINTICINCO

It was early morning in Havana and still pitch dark outside Abuela's apartment. She had woken early, dressed quickly, and now sat in her rocking chair praying her morning rosary. Her thoughts wandered to her family in the United States. She hoped Luisito was able to carry out the mission. It was crucial that he delivered this message. But she feared that he would be dazzled with all the new and wonderful things the United States had to offer and wouldn't be aware of the urgency of the message. It was awful how she couldn't remind him in her letters. She had placed a few calls to the United States, but after she had spoken to Maricusa she hadn't been able to communicate again. Abuela tried to concentrate on her prayers and ask the Blessed Mother to help her.

When she finished praying, Abuela walked out the door quietly. She knew the way out of the building with her eyes closed. As she opened the front door of the building, the knob almost fell off in her hand. What a shame! They had cared so much for this house. Now everything was falling apart and there were no parts for repairs.

It was a constant pain and struggle for her to remember how beautiful her country had once been. She closed the door and slowly walked the two blocks to Lola's home. Lola, her neighbor and friend, used to be a beauty shop owner. She now secretly worked from her home, trimming ladies' hair in exchange for whatever extra food or favors they could provide. There was something more important here than the haircut Abuela was about to get. She used this opportunity to exchange information with the other women or buy food from the black market. This was the only way to survive in Cuba.

She tapped on Lola's window, and a curvy lady in her sixties opened the door. Abuela hurried in and gave her a kiss. Today Lola was wearing curlers in her hair. She greeted Abuela with a brush and comb in hand.

"Maria Elena, *qué bueno verte*," Lola said. "It's so nice to see you! Come on in."

Inside the dim dining room two other people awaited them: Fefa Rodriguez, the farmer's wife, and Mati Valdes, Abuela's former housekeeper. It was odd how the three women of different upbringings and political beliefs had bonded in these times of trouble. Lola and Mati were active in the Communist Party, but Abuela never spoke to them about politics, nor did she know if they were truly believers or just participated to survive. The women knew one another from way back, and their friendship and respect for each other was stronger than anything else.

Fefa was not there just to have her hair cut either. She had a bag with mangos, potatoes, and bananas for Abuela. In order to survive, Fefa and her husband would separate some of the fruits and other crops they grew on their farm from what they had to hand over to the government. They would sell or barter them to the people they knew. This had to be done in a secure place at odd times so they wouldn't be caught. It was forbidden to have any side businesses that the government didn't control.

"Maria Elena, I brought you a few goodies," Fefa said to Abuela, handing her a canvas bag with the food. She knew Abuela would later return the bag with money or some useful object.

Abuela had brought a piece of linen fabric, which she gave to Lola in exchange for a haircut. Lola washed Abuela's hair in the kitchen sink and proceeded to trim her hair in front of the living room mirror. If anyone knocked on the door the house would resemble a normal apartment with no trace of a beauty shop. Even women like Mati, who had ties to the government, would keep the secret about the beauty shop. After all, the women needed a haircut, and they could get one at Lola's house without waiting in any lines.

"*¡Qué calor hace!*" Lola said, fanning herself with a newspaper. "I can't believe it is still hot during the day in November!"

"You must miss your family very much," Mati commented.

"Yes, you know how young people are," Abuela said, pretending she had never known of her family's plan to leave the island. "They have other ideas in their head, you know, like birdies flying around. *¡Están locos!*"

"Yes, it was crazy to risk their lives like that," Mati replied.

"Enough said about that. I am here alone and I have to get used to it," Abuela said. Then, changing the subject she asked, "Did anyone hear the four o'clock *novela* yesterday on the radio?"

The conversation turned to the romance of Julieta and Rolando in the latest radio soap called *Amor sin Barreras*, Love without Barriers.

Mati went to the kitchen to get some water as the conversation continued in the dining room. Abuela excused herself and followed her. Mati met her halfway down the corridor.

"Señora, as cook in the house of the Minister of Foreign Affairs in Cuba, I hear many things. They speak freely in front of me. I am most trusted," she said, giving herself an air of importance.

"Of course," Abuela said, knowing Mati wanted to show her how important she was in her new job.

"As I was saying, my bosses think highly of me, and I hear them speak of many things," Mati continued.

"I'm sure and . . . ?" Abuela said, trying to nudge some information from her.

"They are very worried, especially about the younger people. They are afraid that they will storm the foreign embassies just to leave the island," she said.

"You've told me this before," Abuela said. "Is it for sure?"

"Don't say a word about this," Mati said in a whisper, looking both ways as she spoke. "I think this will happen soon and the Cuban government is not going to stop them."

"How is that?" Abuela said.

"I heard them say it was a good opportunity to get rid of troublemakers," she said.

"Hmm," Abuela said. "I guess it makes sense."

"Oh, by the way, my employers gave this to me," Mati said, handing Abuela writing paper from under her apron. "I kept one pack but I really don't have much use for the others."

It was a whole package of thin, yellow, lined Cuban paper, *papel cebolla*—onion skin, Abuela liked to say. It was just what she needed to write to her family.

"*Gracias*, Mati," she said. Whether Mati still felt affection toward Abuela, or just wanted to show that she was important, Abuela was most grateful.

# 26 VEINTISÉIS

Luisito walked downstairs slowly. He wondered if he was actually doing the right thing. But who better to trust than Rosie, who had been so kind to him and his parents? Downstairs he found José sleeping in the reclining chair and Rosie glued to the TV set.

"Tía Rosa, I need to talk to you," Luisito said as he sat beside her.

"What's the matter, Luisito? Are you hungry?" she asked. "We have plenty of leftovers in the refrigerator."

"No, no, it's not that," Luisito said.

"A girl problem?" she said with a smile.

"No, not that either," Luisito said, grinning. "It's about Abuela."

"Oh, my dear," she said, reaching out to pat his hand, "I know how you must worry about your dear grandmother, but she is not as frail as she may look. We are working on getting her papers so she can join us soon."

"It's not that," Luisito said. "Please, don't tell anyone. You promise?"

"Oh, my, Luisito," she said now sitting up, "you have my attention. What is it?"

"Abuela needs me to get something done for Cuba. She is counting on me to accomplish something in Miami and I need your help," he said. He told her the whole story, relieved that it was out in the open.

"Wow, your Abuela is really something!" Rosie said. *"¡Increíble!"*

"Why do you say it's incredible?" Luisito said.

"She doesn't ever give up. No matter her age or how many obstacles there are," Rosie said. "She is a fighter!"

"Please don't tell anyone," Luisito said. "Tommy and Sonia know, but no one else can find out."

"Why can't you ask your parents?" Rosie asked.

"Abuela told me not to tell anyone, and I think she was afraid that my parents would not let me get involved. They were always afraid in Cuba that it could be dangerous for me," Luisito said.

"Are you afraid now, Luisito?" Rosie said.

"No," Luisito said, very confident. "Abuela taught me that if you are sure you are doing the right thing you don't need to be afraid."

"Yes, but . . ." Rosie started to say.

"Abuela says the Bible is full of quotes telling us not to be afraid," Luisito added.

"Abuela taught you a lot about the Bible, didn't she?"

"Not really. She taught me mostly with her example," Luisito said. "My parents didn't want her to have a Bible around the house or say things to me that I would repeat to others and get in trouble."

Rosie let out a big sigh of resignation. "Let me think more about how I can get you to Miami. Don't worry, we won't let Abuela down."

"It's for Cuba," Luisito said, smiling.

"That's right!" Rosie said. Luisito gave her a kiss, glanced at José, who was still sound asleep, and ran upstairs, feeling much better.

*¡Ay, mi Dios querido!* Rosie said to herself. *My dear God, how am I going to get Luisito to Miami without telling his parents the whole story? I'm going to have to do a lot of praying so you can show me the way!*

The next morning was Sunday. Luisito woke up early, eager to go to Mass. He felt happier and almost lighter, as if a big weight had been taken from his shoulders.

The family headed to church together. Luisito understood the Mass much better each time he went. His favorite part of the Mass was when the priest elevated the Holy Eucharist and the bell rang.

On the way to Mass, he looked at some of the neighbors' cars parked in front of the house. They were probably sleeping in. Imagine being allowed to go to Mass and just not wanting to go, he thought. How different from Cuba! So many people there wanted to go but felt it was too dangerous.

"Tommy, why do you suppose Steve and Allen don't go to Mass? Are they Catholic?" Luisito asked.

"Yeah, but they are lazy. They go once in a while," Tommy said.

"But I learned in the catechism classes I'm now going to that it is a sin not to go to Mass on Sunday. It breaks one of the Ten Commandments," Luisito said.

"Maybe they don't know that," Tommy said. "Steve says he can always pray at home."

"But he doesn't receive the Holy Eucharist," Luisito quickly answered.

"Yep, that is true," Tommy said.

Luisito couldn't wait to make his first Holy Communion. He was going to classes and was planning on receiving first Penance and first Communion by Easter of next year.

After Mass, they all went to buy some of the doughnuts that the Boy Scouts were selling in the church parking lot. As Luisito was munching on his glazed doughnut, he felt a tap on his shoulders.

"Hi, Lewis!" Sherry said, smiling.

"Hi!" said Luisito. "I was looking for you before Mass but I didn't see you. Are you coming to the championship basketball game tomorrow?"

"Of course!" Sherry said.

They chatted for a few minutes about the game.

Then Luisito saw Sherry stare at someone in the crowd.

"What is it?" Luisito said.

"Nothing," Sherry said, turning around to see if anyone was posing behind them. No one was there. "I thought I saw a man take a picture of us . . . anyway, what was I saying?"

Luisito and Tommy just looked at each other.

# 27 VEINTISIETE

Luisito walked into the school gym the night of the district championship game. The gym was packed with parents, teachers, students, and relatives—especially Luisito's. Three long rows of family: cousins, great-aunts and -uncles, and his parents were there to cheer him on. They had the same large cameras around their necks that they had worn on the day he had arrived at the airport. Luisito could distinguish their hearty laughs in the din of the crowd. Some of his younger cousins had made maracas out of coffee cans. They rattled them as they cheered.

School spirit was at its best in the gym for the championship. Luisito paused to take it all in. The wood floors looked recently polished. There were large, colorful banners with the blue-and-gold school colors everywhere. As he looked around the gym, for the first time since he had arrived in the United States, Luisito felt he belonged. He was part of something.

They were playing against the undefeated Oakwood High School Tigers. Luisito watched the Tigers warm up. He snapped to attention when he saw Coach Jerry signal all his players to huddle.

"All right, mighty Lions, this year we have a chance to be district champions! Remember, it's not just your skills but your determination that will get us that trophy. Now, do we want to win?" he shouted.

"Yes, we do!" they shouted.

"I can't hear you!" Coach Jerry said.

"Yes, we do!" they shouted louder.

"Well, then, get out there" he said, and sent them out onto the court.

The game started slowly. The ball went back and forth as both teams played great defense. It was still 6–6 by the end of the first quarter.

"Let's start making some shots!" shouted a group of parents.

"Defense! Defense!" shouted others from the packed bleachers.

By the end of the second quarter the Tigers led 20–12. The Lions fans became quieter, attentively watching every pass with hopes of catching up. In the third quarter, the Tigers started to get too confident, and the Lions started scoring. When the score was 24–23, with the Tigers still leading, one of the Lions stole the ball, zigzagged down the court, and made a three-point shot! Now the Lions were leading. But by the end of the third quarter, the score was tied again, 30–30.

As the fourth quarter started, the Lions players' tiredness started to show in their slower running and clumsier passing. All of them had played the whole game so far. Coach Jerry signaled to Luisito.

"Lewis, you're in!" he called. "Give Paul a rest."

Luisito nervously trotted out onto the court. Both teams continued to play well, and when the buzzer rang, the score was tied and the game went into overtime. Luisito was certain that Coach Jerry was going to take him out and put Paul back in, but to his surprise Coach Jerry sent him back out onto the court.

Now it seemed no one could get the ball in the hoop. Luisito could feel his jersey glued to his back with sweat. His face was now bright red, and the once cold gym felt as warm as a day on a Miami beach.

There were only forty seconds on the clock when the referee called a foul against the Lions, and the Tigers made the two penalty shots.

"No more fouls!" Coach Jerry yelled at his players.

Now the Lions had the ball. Eric passed it to Ron, who dribbled in and made a layup, tying the score yet again. They went into defensive mode as the Tigers took off down the court. They moved too fast and went out of bounds, and the Lions had the ball again. Fifteen seconds left.

This time Eric passed the ball to Luisito, but one of the Tigers pushed him and Luisito fell hard on the floor. The referee called a foul, and Luisito had the chance to make two shots. If he made them they would win the game. He felt the pressure almost suffocating him. He could hear faint gasps and Spanish comments from his relatives.

Luisito stood just behind the foul line. He was so nervous! A thousand thoughts swirled through his mind. *You can do it if you just concentrate hard enough. But what will happen if I miss it? Will everyone hate me? They're just starting to warm up to me . . .* He heard shouts of: "Lewis, you can do it!" and "Bend those knees!" He looked toward his parents and saw Miguel cheering him on and his mother covering her face with her hands. He heard a woman's voice calling, *"¡Encomiéndate a Dios, mi hijito!"* It was surely one of his relatives reminding him to say a prayer.

He caught the ball and dribbled it twice. He didn't know if this merited a mental prayer, but he said one anyway. "Dear God, I hope this goes in . . . for my team and for my sake. Please, God, hear my prayer and, if not, let me cope with whatever happens."

Then he shot the ball high in the air and it bounced right off the rim of the basket. There were sighs from one side of the gym and cheers from the other.

The referee bounced the ball back to him and signaled that he had one more chance. He breathed deeply, dribbled just once, bent his knees, and shot the basketball. He didn't even want to watch, so he shut his eyes. When he opened them the ball was spinning around and around the rim of the basket. Finally, it dropped in. Immediately a cheer roared from the crowd, and his teammates charged toward him with hugs and pats on the back. The buzzer rang. The Lions had won by just one point.

His parents and a long line of relatives ran onto the court to congratulate Luisito and each team player.

"Great job, Lewis!" Coach Jerry yelled as he jumped in the air with excitement.

The Lions stepped aside to have their picture taken with a big silver trophy. They let Luisito stand in the center holding the award.

As Luisito turned for more pictures, Sherry came up and gave him a big hug. "You were amazing, Lewis!" she said.

"Well, let's go celebrate!" Coach Jerry said. "Where should we go?"

"How about *El Rincon Cubano*?" Paul suggested. "That's the Cuban restaurant in Silver Spring."

Friends and family paraded out of the school and headed to the restaurant. When they reached the restaurant, the owner had to open up the area reserved for parties in order to seat them all together. Luisito was all smiles. *Thank you, God!* he thought so strongly that he was sure the others could hear him.

# 28 VEINTIOCHO

It was raining and Abuela held a trash bag over her head as she walked to Mass early in the morning. She opened the large wooden doors of *La Iglesia de la Merced,* the Church of Mercy. Although it needed repairs, the church and especially the altar were still breathtaking. Abuela walked toward the confessional and waited in line with two other older ladies. When it was her turn she knelt down and closed the confessional door. Finally, Padre Pepito opened the small grated window that separated them.

"Padre, forgive me, for I have sinned," Abuela said.

"How long since your last confession?" Padre Pepito asked.

"It has been a month," Abuela said. At the end of her confession, she added the phrase that would identify her, "I am sorry for my lack of trust in God but I know I can count on his mercy."

"Oh, yes," Padre Pepito said, recognizing her. "You can count on his mercy. As penance, pray a rosary and meditate on the life of Christ. If I may suggest, you should do this in the rose garden by the statue of Mary."

"*Si, Padre,*" Abuela said as the priest absolved and blessed her.

Abuela left the confessional and looked for the door that led to the rose garden. She prayed the rosary by the statue of Mary as she waited for the priest. She really didn't need to go to confession today, but she did need to speak to Padre Pepito. They had to go through this ritual in case someone overheard them in the confessional. There were rumors that some confessionals were bugged by the government. Once Padre Pepito finished hearing confessions, he walked into the sacristy to put his stole away and then quietly slipped through the door to the rose garden. He walked slowly toward Abuela and gently tapped her on the shoulders.

"*Hola, Padre,*" Abuela said quickly. "Listen to this! The exodus will begin soon."

"Is it confirmed?" Padre Pepito asked.

"Yes," Abuela said. "We just don't know exactly when. What do you know about our Lady?"

"She is on her way," the priest said with a smile.

"Will you ever join your family in Miami, Father?" she asked.

"I can't, Maria Elena," Padre Pepito responded. "If there is anyone whom the government would immediately allow to leave Cuba, it is the priests. But if I leave, who would tend the flock?"

"God bless you, Padre. We certainly need you here," Abuela said, giving the priest a hug.

Abuela left the rose garden feeling assured that things were taken care of.

✦ ✦ ✦

On her way home, she stopped in the side chapel of *La Iglesia de la Merced* to kneel before the image of our Lady of Lourdes. Abuela had gotten married in this church. It was filled with so many happy memories. How she wished she were with her family again! Abuela prayed hard for her family and for her country.

She walked home slowly, occasionally looking back to see if she was being followed. She noticed a strange car parked outside the church. It was the same car that had been parked across the street from her house for two days now with someone inside listening to the radio. She hadn't known if they were watching her or someone else, but now she was certain they were watching her. She decided to avoid the man in the car by going into the *bodeguita.* Besides, the line was long. *They must have meat there today,* she thought. Then she remembered that her friend Miriam lived in the nearby apartments. She hurried across the street and went into Miriam's building. When she saw a door at the end of the complex that led to an alley, she decided to go through the hall and out the back of the building. Cars couldn't make it through the narrow road behind the building. She walked down the alley to the next block, turned, and followed her usual way back home, looking cautiously behind her. Nobody was following. She reached her apartment a bit out of breath. It was too much excitement for an old lady. She only wanted to live in peace.

Her hands were still shaking as she opened the door to her apartment. She closed and locked her door. She heard footsteps, but they stopped, and she heard a door slam. It was just a neighbor. Before she even put down her purse, she looked in her cupboard for a few twigs of *tilo,* linden leaves. She was in luck—she had electricity today. She boiled the soothing herbal tea to calm her nerves and whispered a quick prayer to her guardian angel. *Things will be fine*, she assured herself.

# 29 VEINTINUEVE

Sitting on his bed, Luisito emptied out his book bag. He would start with math homework, which came the easiest to him. Tommy was downstairs raiding the kitchen for snacks. Sonia knocked on his door.

"Meeting in my room in five minutes," she said, gesturing toward it with her glass of chocolate milk.

"Here, do you want a doughnut?" Tommy said, offering a plate to Luisito as he walked into Sonia's room.

"Okay, what's new?" Luisito asked, taking a bite of his doughnut.

"Well, you tell us," Sonia said.

"I spoke to your mom and she said she would find a way," Luisito said.

"Okay, but did she say when?" Sonia asked.

"I haven't had a chance to speak to her again," Luisito said.

He glanced out the window and caught a glimpse of a man with blond hair in a car across the street. He got up to take a closer look. The car drove off suddenly.

"What are you looking at?" Tommy asked.

"I thought I saw that man who seems to be following us," Luisito said.

"Do you think he has anything to do with the secret?" Tommy asked.

"I don't know," Luisito said.

*"La cena está servida,"* Miguel called upstairs.

"Let's go, you heard Dad. Dinner is served," Sonia said. "When I'm nervous I get very hungry."

Everyone took his or her seat at the table and they said a prayer. Then they began passing around the fluffy white rice, juicy pork, and steaming black beans. There were also sweet golden plantains.

"You know, Tía Rosie," Luisito said as they ate, "I just saw that car that passes by often."

"And we keep seeing people following us," Tommy added.

"Have you written down the license plate number of the car?" José asked.

"I got half the number of one car," Luisito said, "but they are quick and it's not just one car. We see different people in different places. Always men."

"You know," Miguel said, "I thought I saw someone looking at me the other day when I was leaving work."

"I will call a friend of mine from the police department and ask him what he thinks," José said.

"He is going to think we are crazy," Sonia said. "Really, Dad?"

"Well, let's not worry too much," Rosie said, looking at Elena with concern. "With so many of us in and out of this house I don't think they can rob us. But maybe you should talk to your friend anyway, José."

"Yes, I will do that," José said.

"Now, I was thinking we could go to Miami for Christmas. What do you all think?" Rosie said, changing the subject quickly. She panned her eyes around the table.

"I don't think I can ask for time off from work," Miguel said.

"José, can you try asking Raulito?" Rosie asked, referring to José's friend who was now Miguel's boss. "Maybe you can tell him it's a family vacation and you need a break."

"If Miguel can come, I think it's a wonderful idea," Elena said.

"We need to tell Abuela Maricusa. Christmas is in a few weeks," Sonia said, breaking a piece of soft Cuban bread.

Luisito ate quietly, not knowing whether to be relieved or nervous that his plan to go to Miami was working out. More than anything, he wanted to fulfill his promise to Abuela, but he was getting the feeling that it was no ordinary message he was about to deliver. He caught his aunt's eye and realized she was thinking the same thing.

# 30 TREINTA

Abuela went to the *bodeguita* to get her ration of food for the month. The line wasn't that long today. She stood there chatting with the neighbors about the weather and the latest gossip about who was getting married and who was divorcing whom. There wasn't much else that was safe to talk about in Cuba.

When it was Abuela's turn she presented her ration book and was given her small bag of rice and beans and twenty slices of bread. This meant that there were some days she wouldn't eat bread or she would have to cut the slices in half to make it last longer.

She took a back way home to her apartment building. She looked back a few times, but she wasn't being followed. She guessed that the government had given up on her. *They finally realize my life is too boring,* Abuela mused. The thought made her laugh.

Abuela took a siesta on the bed that used to be Elena's and Miguel's. She awoke to the laughter and singing of people walking in the streets. She missed her family. She decided to go to church and pray her rosary in the chapel. Maybe she would even see the priest and have a chance to chat.

She walked out of the building and down the road. A lovely November breeze swept her face. It gave her a chill. She put on the thin black sweater she was carrying.

*La Iglesia de la Merced* was around the corner. This place was her oasis, her haven. She walked in, made the sign of the cross, and scanned the church. There was only one other elderly woman praying the rosary. The elderly who didn't work were the only ones who were somewhat free to go to church, because they couldn't be fired from work or ridiculed at school.

Abuela sat in one of the pews in front of the statue of our Lady of Lourdes, and she started to pray the rosary. After a while she saw the other lady leave. When she was praying the third joyful mystery she suddenly noticed a shadow in front of her. Then from behind her pew a hand reached over and grabbed onto her shoulder. She looked down at it before she turned around. It was heavy and big—definitely a man's hand. *Probably a beggar,* she thought.

"Maria Elena," said a hoarse voice.

She turned around and stared directly into the face of the man who had been following her.

"Please take your hand off me," she said sternly. The man promptly removed his hand. She could see his face clearly, and she was certain it was the man who had been watching her apartment.

"Do you know these people?" he said, taking out pictures of Luisito playing basketball in front of Rosie's house.

"Oh, Luisito!" Abuela said, taking the pictures.

"I just want you to know that we are keeping an eye on your family. You know us and what we are capable of doing. We are everywhere," the man said, stressing the last few words.

Abuela was not one who was easily intimidated, and although she wanted to cry, she swallowed hard and faked a smile.

"Do you have more?" she asked. "I haven't seen him for months."

The man stared hard at her for a moment and then threw the pictures on her lap and left.

Abuela took a deep breath. She sat in the pew fingering the pictures and finishing her rosary. She didn't have the strength to get up. Her legs were trembling. She always tried to remain strong in front of the communists, those intolerant dictators. She felt the heat rising to her cheeks. She went from feeling scared to angry to courageous.

She stared at the pictures of Luisito happily playing basketball with friends. He was dressed so well and looked so healthy. He even had brand-new American sneakers just like the ones he had always dreamed of. Abuela walked home slowly. No one was following her. When she got home she went straight to her bedroom, closed the door, and started to weep, shaken by the experience. She prayed that they wouldn't hurt her family. She might be old, but she knew that she wasn't someone they wanted to reckon with.

# 31 TREINTA Y UNO

The days seemed so long for FBI Agent John Stewart. He trailed Jorge and Antonio all day and sometimes long into the night until his replacement took over. These men had been seen with some others who were suspected of having ties with the Cuban government. After a few calls and some background checks, Agent Stewart discovered that the men did not have full-time jobs. Yet they often visited nightclubs and expensive restaurants, and occasionally went on shopping sprees. Who—or what—was financing their lavish lifestyle? Was it drugs, counterfeit money, or burglary?

Or could they be Cuban spies? Agent Stewart was part of the Foreign Counterintelligence Squad of the FBI, better known as the FCI. He had often followed Cubans as they spied on prominent Cuban exiles. He had an advantage in his Anglo looks—blond hair, fair complexion, slight freckles, and blue eyes—that belied his fluency in Spanish. He had been raised in the Spanish-speaking neighborhood of New Jersey's Union City and understood the language perfectly. Even in crowded elevators or on buses people spoke freely in Spanish in front of him, never suspecting that someone who looked like him would understand anything they were saying.

Sometimes spies infiltrated Cuban exile organizations in Florida pretending they were just regular citizens. Agent Stewart and his men watched them closely until they had hard facts that warranted an arrest. Other times these spies would participate in demonstrations and act disorderly just to give the exile community a bad name. But if these men were spies, why were they stalking this ordinary family in the suburbs of Maryland?

The information Agent Stewart had on the Galleti family raised no red flags. José Galleti was a Cuban architect who owned his own firm. His wife, Rosie, worked with him as office manager. They had two children, Sonia and Thomas, who attended Big Spring High School. They weren't involved in anything political and had no active records or police files. Rosie had family who had just arrived from Cuba, Miguel and Elena Ramirez and their son, Luis. They had also been regular citizens in Cuba. They had not even been active members of the Communist party. Day after day, Agent Stewart observed how the men drove by the Galleti home, Miguel's workplace, and the high school. They were definitely after this particular family. The question was, why? There was really no logical reason—yet.

This case had to be handled very carefully. He could not arrest anyone just for driving by someone's house or for bumping into someone more than once in a public place. He and his men were following their trail everywhere now. Recently he had even pretended he was a reporter at Luisito's basketball games just to keep an eye on the spies and on the family.

Today was the perfect morning to check out the spies' rented apartment in Baltimore. What criminal activity were these men up to? He parked his car a block away. With a warrant in his pocket, he walked into the lobby, dressed casually to blend in with the other resisdents. The complex had several apartments, and because the renters changed often, the residents didn't know one another very well. So no one questioned him as he walked right to the apartment as if it were his own. He knocked several times on the door of apartment 212 but no one was home. He took out a master key and tried it. *Click*. The door opened. The apartment smelled of tobacco combined with some kind of perfumed incense.

He went toward the kitchen. There were dirty dishes stacked in the sink. In the living room, he placed a bugging device inside one of the chrome legs of the coffee table.

He looked around the bedroom. In one corner he saw a small transistor radio, the kind that could be used to communicate with Cuba. On the other side of the room two large duffle bags were piled one on top of the other. From the amount of luggage they had, it seemed the men would not be in the country for very long. They probably packed light so that they could move quickly. A makeshift clothesline in the walk-in closet held several black and white photos as they dried. Some were of Luis and his friends at school, others were of Rosie and Elena at stores, of Miguel leaving his workplace, and of the front of the Galleti's house. The only other room in the apartment had a sign: *No entre*—Do not enter. That must be where they developed their rolls of film. Agent Stewart did not enter the room. He didn't want to alert them by possibly exposing any film.

He saw little paperwork around, so he couldn't get any information that way. Then he saw a photo of the image of Our Lady of Charity in a Cuban church. He knew this was his first clue. These men wouldn't have this picture with them for prayer. There was something important about this image, and he needed to find out what.

# 32 TREINTA Y DOS

The night before they left, Luisito's family loaded the car with all their suitcases. They were ready to leave for Miami. Miguel's boss had given him some time off. Luisito and Rosie had their plan all worked out. Once they arrived, Rosie would find an excuse to take Luisito to *La Ermita de la Caridad* in Miami. There he would quickly deliver his message. It's a good thing he had decided to tell Rosie—this was turning out to be easier than he'd expected.

Early the next morning, the whole family crammed into the car. José, Rosie, and Sonia took the spacious vinyl front seat. Miguel, Elena, Luisito, and Tommy sat in the back.

"I brought coffee and my favorite crackers!" Rosie said.

"Well, then we are all set," José laughed.

Luisito rested his head back and slept as his parents and the Galletis spoke softly.

After several hours, they stopped at a rest area.

"Finally, we get to stretch our legs," Tommy said.

*"No importa,"* Luisito said. "Try a raft for about four days."

"Well, now that you put it that way . . ." Tommy said, smiling.

They bought a quick breakfast and brought it back to the car to eat. Between the food and the moving vehicle, Luisito slowly drifted in and out of sleep. He would soon be in Miami. But instead of a sense of accomplishment, he felt uneasy about the whole thing.

It just couldn't be this easy. Something wasn't right.

✦ ✦ ✦

Agent Stewart drank his cup of coffee as he drove on the highway en route to Miami. He picked up his portable radio.

"Yes?" Stewart said. "What do you have?"

"Agent Stewart, the wiretaps indicate that the two Cuban suspects are after an image of Our Lady of Charity, and they believe the boy has something to do with it. Apparently his family has connections with the Catholic Church in Cuba, and, as we know, the Cuban government is very afraid that the Catholic Church, always against injustice, will try to bring the government down," his assistant said.

"But according to inside information the boy's parents didn't go to church. They weren't affiliated with the Church at all," Stewart replied.

"Correct, but the boy also lived with his grandmother, and she went to church daily. That's all the information we have so far," she said.

"The grandmother is still in Cuba, isn't she?" Stewart asked.

"Yes, she is seventy-two years old and lives in Havana."

"There is nothing suspicious about an old lady going to church in Cuba. The older people have nothing to lose," he said. "Keep digging and keep me posted."

This whole thing didn't make sense to Stewart. Why would anyone be so concerned about a holy image? Were they afraid the teenage boy was going to smuggle this image to the United States? How could he if he came in a raft with no personal belongings? His parents had no involvement with anticommunist movements, the Church, or any communist groups, according to his information. Then there was the grandmother, but all she did was stand in line for food, visit old friends, and go to church. He had checked out the people she visited and they were just ordinary folks.

He heard Agent Loynaz on the radio again. He tried to set down his coffee. It spilled on his lap.

"Y-e-s?" he said, a little irritated.

"Just wanted to let you know that the family is forty miles ahead of you and still being closely followed," said Carmen Loynaz, an agent assigned to FCI.

"Do you have someone on them?"

"Yes, we do."

"Good," Stewart reported. "I will soon be entering South Carolina. Where are they now?"

"Approaching Georgia," Agent Loynaz said.

"Okay, I'd better pick up the pace," Stewart said. "Thanks."

Stewart turned up the radio and sped up a bit. This was a lonely job at times. Everything was top secret. He remembered how his father, who had also worked for the bureau, would leave for days on account of his work. Stewart's father was an FBI legend. He was known for his highly intuitive sharp mind, his amazing high-speed car chases, and his many successfully closed cases. His father was in more fragile health since his hip replacement surgery, but he had once been a very agile man.

"Wait a minute," Stewart said to himself. His father might be fragile now, but he was really something in his day . . . "That's it!" He radioed Agent Loynaz again.

"The reports you have of Maria Elena Jemot, are they all recent?" he asked.

"From the last ten years," she said.

"Check further back," Stewart said, "during the years right after the revolution. Check her husband as well. I believe he was an attorney who was arrested and died in prison."

"Will do," Loynaz said. "Keep your eyes open."

"I will, thanks," he said, signing off.

This is the part of his job he enjoyed the most. It could be boring for days, but then one clue and—bingo!—

the information started to pour in. He was glad he had such a good team working for him. He hoped this hunch panned out because he had a feeling this was no routine assignment.

# 33 TREINTA Y TRES

Antonio and Jorge had seen the Galleti and Ramirez families loading suitcases into their car the night before they left for Miami. Early the next morning, the spies were waiting on a side street, ready to follow them. Now they sped down the highway after them, keeping a safe distance so as not to arouse suspicion. It was a good thing they had borrowed someone else's car.

"You know, Jorge, that old woman, Maria Elena Jemot, is a sneaky old lady," said Antonio, laughing. "You've got to hand it to her."

"She is slick, all right," Jorge said cynically. "I don't know how she does it. Maybe it's all that praying she does. She has some superior being protecting her."

"What do you think she asked her relatives to do?" Antonio said.

"I don't know, but I have a feeling that we'll find our answers in Miami," Jorge said. "Look, they're stopping in this rest area."

Antonio swerved into the side lane to go into the rest stop.

"Let's get more coffee," Antonio said. "I am beat."

"I should be sleeping while you drive so we can switch later," Jorge said.

"Okay, stay in the car. I will get coffee for myself," he said, putting on his sunglasses and pulling the hood of his jacket over his head so no one would recognize him.

✦ ✦ ✦

Only ten miles away Agent Stewart was talking again with Agent Loynaz.

"We found a lead to some interesting information," Agent Loynaz said. "The grandmother, Maria Elena Jemot, was in favor of the revolution right at the beginning, like many others. But as soon as the government declared themselves socialist she started peacefully working underground with the Catholic Church."

"Interesting," Stewart said. "I knew there was something more to this lady."

"She helped seminarians and people trying to get off the island, and was instrumental in the Pedro Pan movement," she said.

"Hmm, Operation Pedro Pan," Stewart said, "when 14,000 Cuban children were smuggled out of Cuba to escape communism and were taken care of in this country by the Catholic Church . . ."

"I will keep researching and let you know of any new developments," Loynaz said.

"All right, thanks," Stewart said and continued driving.

# 34 TREINTA Y CUATRO

After another stop, Sonia took the wheel until evening. Then Rosie continued driving until they arrived in Miami.

"We are not far," Tommy said to Luisito.

"How long?" Luisito said.

"I don't know, but we are close. When I see palm trees I know we are getting close to my Abuela Maricusa," Tommy said.

"I hope she is waiting for us with hot chocolate and *churros*," Sonia said.

"What are *churros*? A typical Miami food?" Luisito asked.

"No, they're a pastry eaten in Cuba with hot chocolate or *café con leche*. It's really from Spain, but many countries claim it because it is so good!" Rosie said.

"I remember eating *churros* as a child," Elena said. "In fact, I had forgotten all about them until now."

"You are going to love them," Tommy told Luisito who by now was quite hungry just thinking about it.

It was already dark when they drove through the streets of Miami. They saw mostly one-story ranch homes with aluminum fencing.

"Look, Abuela and Abuelo are waiting for us on the porch!" Tommy exclaimed.

As expected, hugs and kisses and hot chocolate awaited them. *My cousins were right*, Luisito thought. The hot thick chocolate was delicious, especially when he dipped the *churro* into it. Maricusa had guest rooms prepared for the parents and the sunroom ready with cots and sleeping bags for the kids. Luisito, exhausted from the excitement and the long day, fell asleep in seconds.

The next morning Luisito woke to the strong aroma of Cuban coffee and cheerful noises coming from the kitchen: the percolating of the coffeemaker, the sizzling of *huevo fritos* (fried eggs), the popping of the toaster, and the constant opening and closing of the refrigerator. It was breakfast time, all right!

"After lunch let's go to the grocery store to get some things," Maricusa said to Rosie.

"No, Mami," Rosie said, sensing her chance. "Make me a list and I will go with the kids. You can stay here and continue cooking."

"Do you remember where the grocery store is?" Manuel, Tommy's grandfather, asked her.

"Of course I remember," Rosie said.

Meanwhile, the family ate breakfast and chatted about Christmas, about the process of obtaining Abuela's immigration papers, and, of course, what to do when Cuba was free again.

"I'll go back to live in my house in *el barrio* of Milagros in Havana," Maricusa sighed.

"Ah! It's probably a *cuarteria*, a squatter home, all in disrepair thanks to the revolution!" José said.

"You are absolutely right, I've passed by it," Elena said.

"I will buy a vacation beach home in Varadero. I will renovate it and spend my summers there, but I'm not going back there to live," Rosie said. "The United States is my home now."

"Hey, stop dreaming for a minute and come outside to look at the *gallinas*, the hens," Manuel said to Rosie. "This is where I got the eggs you just had for breakfast."

"Only in Miami can you have chickens as pets in your backyard," José said, laughing.

Rosie followed her father out the door to see the hens. But she missed the last step and fell to the ground. Her flip-flops flew into the air. She cried out in pain.

"*¡La niña se cayó!*" Manuel shouted.

"Who fell?" Tommy said.

"Your mother! Quick, get some ice!" Manuel said.

"Honey, are you okay?" José asked.

"I think I sprained my ankle," Rosie said.

José helped her to the sofa and put her feet up.

"Bring the ice," Maricusa said. "She will be fine."

"Now, don't do anything. Just rest," Miguel said.

The family gathered around her, staring in concern at her foot with a bag of ice on it.

"Well, Sonita," Maricusa said, "you will have to go to the supermarket and pick up the food I need."

"No, I'll go," Rosie said, trying to get up. This was the perfect chance to take Luisito to the shrine of Our Lady of Charity and speak to the priest in charge.

"No way, honey," José said. "You can't go like that. I will go to the grocery store."

Luisito realized this was their only opportunity to go to see the priest.

"I will go with Sonia," he blurted out.

"Let's go!" Sonia said quickly.

"Wait," Rosie said, trying to think quickly. "Give me a piece of paper so I can write down the driving directions for her."

"There's no need. I will just tell her," Maricusa said. "It's really easy. You take this road down to ninety-eighth street. Then you take. . . ."

"Mami, let me write it for her," Rosie said.

Sonia gave her mother a piece of paper. Rosie wrote on it while the family all discussed the easiest way to get to the grocery store.

"Come here," Rosie said. "Let me give you a kiss."

"They're only going to the grocery store," laughed José. "You'd think they were embarking on a dangerous journey."

"Oh, be quiet," Rosie said, forcing a smile. *Ay, Dios mio, what am I doing?* she thought.

# 35 TREINTA Y CINCO

Sonia, Tommy, and Luisito rushed to the car before anyone could have a change of mind.

"Why do you all have to go?" José asked. "Tommy, you stay, and let's help Abuelo with the lawn."

"I want to go with them," Tommy said. "I'll help when I come back."

"Yeah, right," José said. "Those kids will probably end up at the mall. They won't be back right away."

"Oh, let them have fun!" Maricusa said. "They'll only be young once."

Sonia backed the car out and drove two blocks to the nearest stop sign. She pulled over and opened the paper her mother had given them. The paper was folded like a greeting card. It had directions to the grocery store on the front, and on the inside it had instructions on how to get to the shrine.

"This is easy," Sonia said. "I've never driven to the shrine, but I've come every time we visit. It's right by Mercy Hospital. There are signs pointing to the hospital all over the main road. Super easy!"

"Okay, well, let's get it done," Tommy said.

Luisito couldn't feel completely calm until he had delivered his message. He hoped it would benefit Abuela or Cuba somehow.

Following the directions on the paper, they arrived at the shrine with only one or two wrong turns. The pathway to the shrine was lined with royal palm trees. Luisito stopped in awe as he gazed at the architecturally unique church with the ocean as a backdrop. They walked up several steps toward the light blue cone-shaped building that resembled the silhouette of the statue of Our Lady of Charity with her triangular dress. Upon entering, Luisito immediately noticed the large painted mural behind the altar. It was an illustration of the history of Cuba with portraits of patriots, founding fathers, and saints. In the center, the Blessed Mother held the child Jesus. The priest's chair was made of Cuban palm trees. Under the altar, in the foundation of the building, sand from each of the six Cuban provinces was buried.

He saw several groups of people kneeling and looking at the tabernacle while their lips moved silently, as if they were holding a private conversation with God or the Blessed Mother. Many clutched rosaries, as he had often seen Abuela do back in Cuba.

A short nun in a gray habit saw them watching the people and approached them.

"Many people find hope here," she said. "They pray to be reunited with their families. They pray for a free Cuba."

Luisito nodded, still watching the people. He knew exactly how they felt.

"Can I help you?" the nun proceeded to ask.

Luisito focused on what he had come to do. He asked the nun if they could see the Cuban priest.

"I believe he is resting," the nun said. "Father René de Jesús is not as young as he used to be, and it is a very busy time of year."

But Luisito couldn't take no for an answer.

"He is expecting me," he said, bluffing. Maybe he wasn't lying, he thought. The priest could very well be expecting him for all he knew. "I bring him an important message from Cuba," he added.

"Well . . . come with me then. I'll see if he's in," the nun said, eyeing him doubtfully.

They went to an office in the entrance to the shrine, where she made a phone call. She mumbled something to the person on the other end of the phone, then looking at Luisito she asked, "What's your name?"

"My name is Luis Ramirez Jemot. I am Maria Elena Jemot's grandson. I recently arrived from Cuba by raft."

The nun's features softened as she realized he was a Cuban rafter. She whispered into the phone again. Then she hung up the receiver and motioned for them to follow her. They went outside and downstairs to some offices beneath the chapel. They walked down a hall and into a small office with a desk, a phone, two chairs, and many pictures hanging along the wall. A colorfully painted wooden plaque of Our Lady of Charity stood out.

"Please wait here for Father René de Jesús. He will be right with you," she said, pointing to the chairs.

"Is that Father René de Jesús?" Luisito pointed to a picture on the wall.

"Yes, that was taken on the day he was ordained. The woman in the picture is his mother. She passed away a few years ago. A very nice and holy woman."

The nun walked away, closing the door behind her. Her words echoed in Luisito's mind. The priest's mother had passed away. Then who was the mother who was waiting for him in Italy?

At that moment a gray-haired man dressed in black came through the door. A gold cross hung around his neck. With a kind smile he asked, "Who is Maria Elena's grandson?"

"I am," Luisito said, "and these are my cousins. I arrived recently by raft from Cuba. I live in Maryland now, but my abuela told me to deliver an important message to you."

Luisito was so anxious to fulfill his promise that he didn't even give the priest a chance to sit down.

The priest interrupted Luisito by stretching out his hand and shaking Luisito's.

"Father René de Jesús Suarez, a servant of God and yours," he said, pulling Luisito into an embrace.

"I last saw you when you were a baby," he said, to Luisito's surprise. "We received word after you left the island and we prayed for your safe journey."

The priest then shook everyone else's hand as he explained how he had known Luisito's grandparents for many years. He had been in the seminary with his great-uncle, Abuela's brother, who had died before Luisito was born.

"You should be proud of your grandparents, especially of your abuela, who, after your grandfather's death, continued to help her people through the Church."

Luisito took a deep breath. He had waited so long to deliver this message for Abuela. He only hoped he had made it in time. "My abuela told me it was very important to tell you the Scripture verse Exodus 32:1–35. She also told me that your mother is waiting for you in Italy. This is what she told me before our escape, but I don't understand. The nun just told me that the lady in this picture is your mother and that she passed away several years ago."

The priest paced up and down, pondering Luisito's message.

"I understand what she means about my mother," he said. "I don't understand the Exodus part. I'll have to think about that."

The priest explained that he was aware that there was a plan to smuggle an original replica of the statue of Our Lady of Charity from Cuba to the United States through the Italian embassy. Arrangements had been made to bring the statue to the exiles in Miami, but he didn't know it had already been accomplished.

"Why did they have to smuggle the statue? Why couldn't they just make another replica?" Tommy interrupted the priest.

"Well, it wouldn't be the same," Father René de Jesús said. "This statue was carried in a procession around the island every year. It is from Cuba, and bringing her from the island means a lot to Cubans."

"I guess the statue is an exile just like us!" Luisito said.

"Yes, to Cubans the statue represents more than their faith. It also represents their heritage," Father René de Jesús said. "The fact that it is coming from Cuba, where they left everything behind, is very symbolic. She represents protection, unity, peace, and hope—everything Cuban exiles are praying for."

He paced around...

"I can't imagine what your abuela is trying to tell us with the quote from Exodus," he said, rubbing his chin.

"Maybe she is telling us that a tornado is coming and parting the seas," Tommy suggested.

"He is definitely not a prophet," Sonia murmured, shaking her head.

"Well, why not?" Tommy said. "Did *you* come up with anything?"

"I don't think your abuela means it literally," the priest said thoughtfully.

"Whatever it is," Luisito said, "she wants us to be prepared. It was very important for her that I deliver the message."

"Maybe she means . . ." Tommy started to say, but he was immediately interrupted by Sonia.

"Don't even try," Sonia said, holding his elbow.

"I was going to say," Tommy insisted, "that maybe something is coming from Cuba besides the statue."

"I have an idea," Luisito said. "Maybe a lot of Cubans are coming, like a mass exodus! Could that be it?"

"Wait a minute," Sonia said. "You think that the message is that Cubans will be coming to America by sea? If they could have, they would have done that a long time ago."

"There has been a lot of unrest in the island lately. Maybe she means there will be many more rafters . . . or that someone is planning something we don't know about yet," the priest answered. "We don't know how or when—but we have to be prepared."

The group heard a knock on the door, and the nun came in to relay the message that there had been a change of plan. The image, she said, had been secretly given to someone in the Panamanian embassy in Cuba. The man entrusted with making sure the statue was delivered safely would be arriving at the airport that afternoon.

At that moment, the phone rang. The nun answered; then she turned to the priest. "Two more Cubans are here asking to see you. They say they know about the statue, too," she said with a puzzled expression.

"Tell them to come in," Father René de Jesús said.

Moments later, a knock sounded on the door and two men walked into the room.

"Oh, my!" Sonia gasped.

"These men have been following us!" Luisito yelled in Spanish.

"Calm down, we are with the FBI," Antonio lied. "You all speak Spanish?" he asked. Everyone nodded, so he proceeded in that language.

"We have been informed that a statue of some kind is coming into the country. We ourselves are being followed by Cuban spies who are looking for this statue, and we don't understand why there is so much interest in it," he said. "Is it carrying anything inside?"

"No, it's simply a statue," the priest said, trying to downplay the situation.

"When is it arriving?" Antonio asked.

"Today," Luisito admitted and immediately regretted it. Could they really trust these men?

"If you are going to pick it up, we will go with you," he said. "What time will it arrive?"

"In about two hours," the priest replied, glancing at his watch. "Can you please show us your identification?"

"Yes, yes, later. We have no time to waste. We must be on our way," Antonio said. "Because there is such interest in this statue from Cubans of all political beliefs, it is best you all stay behind for your own safety," he continued. "Just tell us who exactly is bringing the statue and we will escort this person."

Father René de Jesús paused. "Hmmm . . . A man in a red shirt will arrive on a plane at Terminal I."

"Easy to find. Thank you—and don't worry, *Padrecito*. We will be back with the statue," Antonio said. The two left quickly, slamming the door behind them.

# 36 TREINTA Y SEIS

Early in the morning, Abuela walked to Lola's house. She needed to trade some items for potatoes. She was very scared this morning, more than she had ever been, for she knew that the government was keeping a close eye on her. Although she hadn't seen anyone following her since the incident at church with the photos, she was still cautious. Ofelia from the *comité de barrio* had probably been warned. Of course, if they did see her go to Lola's house it wouldn't raise a red flag, for she had been visiting Lola for years.

She knocked on the door. Lola answered with her seemingly ever-present curlers in her hair.

"Come in, please," she said, giving Abuela a kiss on the cheek.

The same group of people were there as before. Fefa gave Abuela a bag of potatoes. In exchange, Abuela gave her an old curtain she had found. Fefa could use the fabric to make herself much-needed clothes.

"As soon as I can sneak more vegetables, I will bring them your way," Fefa promised.

The women chatted a little. But Abuela was tired and soon said her good-byes. As she was walking out, Mati confronted her.

"Señora Jemot," Mati said. She hadn't called her that since she had worked for her family as a housekeeper. "Do you miss your family?" she asked, looking sincere.

"Terribly," Abuela said.

"I hope one day you can be reunited with them. You know, that they come to their senses and return," she said nervously.

"Of, course," Abuela said.

Mati looked particularly nervous, as if she wanted to say something but was too afraid. Abuela could sense the conflict in her between her realization that the Communist Party was not living up to her expectations, and her pride of not wanting to admit to her friends that she had made a terrible mistake by supporting the party in the first place.

Abuela patted Mati on the shoulder as she left. She slowly walked the two blocks back to her house. She finally arrived at her building and walked into her apartment. She wished she could continue walking to church, but she was tired. The days seemed so long without her family. She decided to see if the water was running. Maybe a shower would help her feel better. Just as she finished dressing, she heard a knock at the door. *Who could it be?* she wondered. It was just past noon, and most of her neighbors were eating or taking their siestas.

She put on her shoes and tried to look through the peephole. Over time it had become so blurred she could hardly recognize who was on the other side.

"Who is it?" she asked.

"It's me, Señora Jemot," Mati said.

Abuela opened the door quickly. Mati looked scared and serious. She had sweat on her forehead.

"Do you want some water?" Abuela offered.

"Yes, please," Mati said, following Abuela to the small kitchen.

"I have to tell you. As I was preparing lunch yesterday I heard the men I work for mention your grandson. I normally don't listen to their conversations but his name caught my attention. I don't want anything to happen to the boy."

"What did they say about my grandson?" Abuela said, startled.

"I couldn't hear very well, but they said that they were on his trail and that they were close to finding the statue of Our Lady of Charity," she said, catching her breath. "The water, please."

Abuela poured some water into a glass and handed it to her. Mati gulped it down fast.

"Did they say anything else?" Abuela asked.

"Yes, that is why I am here. They said that once they get the statue, you would be dealt with," she said. "I just don't understand why these important government people would be speaking about you, Señora. Your family has always been peaceful, minding your own business."

"Oh, my," Abuela said, sitting down on a stool in the kitchen. Her mind was blank. What could she do now? She couldn't let these cruel people harm her family—especially her dear grandson.

"You have to come with me right now," Mati insisted.

"Where? Should I hide in the church?" she asked.

"No, let's go to the Peruvian embassy," Mati said. "I know the cook there. He is a friend of mine. We'll go there and once we're inside, we'll stay."

"What do you mean 'we'?" Abuela asked.

"There is no time to waste, Señora Jemot. Let's go. I will explain when we get there," she said.

Abuela only had time to pick up her purse, stick two bananas inside, and grab her rosary and important papers. They walked quickly out the door.

# 37 TREINTA Y SIETE

The room was silent after the supposed FBI agents left. Father René de Jesús told Luisito and the others to remain in the office until the statue was brought from the airport, and he excused himself to pray in the chapel.

"Father, those men are not really FBI agents, are they?" Luisito asked the priest quietly before he went to the chapel.

"How did you know?" the priest asked.

"You told them the man bringing the statue would be at Terminal I, but I don't remember seeing that terminal when I was at the airport. You didn't want them to find the right person, did you?"

"No wonder your abuela entrusted you with her message," Father René de Jesús said. "You sure pay attention. The FBI contacted me days ago to be aware of something suspicious regarding the statue of Our Lady of Charity and two Cuban men. I've asked my secretary to call the FBI. Now my son, I must pray. It's the most powerful thing I can do."

Luisito's head was full of questions he had no answers for. He replayed the whole scenario over and over. While the priest went to pray, Luisito could not just wait around. It wasn't in his nature. He paced up and down. Finally he stopped. "We have to do something!" he said to Tommy and Sonia. "Those men are not FBI agents, and they're going to get the statue!"

"They're not FBI? What can we do?" Tommy and Sonia said at the same time.

"We have to find the way to the airport," insisted Luisito.

"Are you going to tell the priest?" Sonia asked.

"Why interrupt him while he is praying? And where did his secretary go?" Luisito said looking around. "Now, if only we had the flight information."

"Does this help?" asked Tommy, holding out a pink sticky note. "It was on the nun's desk. I picked it up and started folding it and I forgot to put it back. It has directions to the airport and the flight information."

"Good!" Luisito said. "Let's go."

They left through a side door and ran to their car.

"When we get to the airport, Tommy, you go talk to security and I will find the men," Luisito said. "We can't let them get away with the statue."

✦ ✦ ✦

At the airport, Antonio and Jorge searched the terminal map in the baggage area, while flight after flight came in. The two men looked at each other, confused. Where could their terminal be?

"Do you see anyone carrying a bag that could fit a small statue?" Antonio asked Jorge.

"I'm looking," Jorge said staring into the crowd. "They would definitely bring it as a carry-on."

Then the passengers from Panama arrived. Among them, Antonio and Jorge noticed the well-known Cuban defector Humberto Gutierrez, who had asked at the Panamanian embassy for political asylum several months earlier.

"Check out the blue bag," Antonio said. "Maybe there is no red shirt. *Me la juego* . . . I bet that guy has the statue in that bag."

"The priest said he would arrive at Terminal I," Jorge insisted.

"I have a strong hunch he was trying to trick us," Antonio said.

"I don't think so," Jorge said.

"I don't trust priests; you know that," Antonio said.

✦ ✦ ✦

Meanwhile, Sonia had dropped Luisito and Tommy off at the airport while she went to look for parking.

Luisito ran toward the international flights. The airport was busy with holiday travelers. He was going against the flow of traffic and kept accidentally bumping into people and their suitcases. Finally, he spotted the two men standing by a column speaking to each other.

He watched as Antonio and Jorge approached a man in his late thirties who was carrying a blue bag. Antonio and Jorge grabbed him by his arms. The other man was taken by surprise. They were speaking quickly and pointing at his bag.

Luisito wondered what was taking Tommy so long. Maybe security didn't believe him. What if Tommy didn't come back? Would he have to watch helplessly as the men took the statue with them?

# 38 TREINTA Y OCHO

Agent Stewart was positioned just outside the terminal and his men were inside, just a few feet from Antonio, Jorge, and Luisito.

Just then, Jorge grabbed the blue bag while Antonio held on to Gutierrez.

"Go now!" Agent Stewart communicated through his radio to the other agents' earpieces.

But out of nowhere, Luisito, who had no idea he was surrounded by FBI agents, ran and grabbed the blue bag right out of the unsuspecting Jorge's hands. Luisito imagined he had just stolen the basketball from his opponent and now he was running straight to the basket. He ran and ran, pushing through the crowd and jumping over luggage.

Antonio and Jorge, stunned, paused for a split second before starting to run after Luisito. This was the opportunity the agents were waiting for, and they wrestled the men to the ground. The agents read the men their rights and handcuffed them.

"Run after the kid with the bag! Quick!" Stewart yelled, not realizing it was Luisito.

Stewart and the agents took off after Luisito.

Luisito was running as fast as he could straight toward security. Stewart caught up to him first.

"It's okay, everyone. He is fine," he said, catching his breath and smiling.

"You okay, kid?" he asked.

"Don't let him grab my bag!" Luisito told the airport security guard. "This man is dangerous. He has been following me for some time."

"Don't worry. I'm with the FBI. I have been protecting you from the Cuban agents," Agent Stewart told Luisito.

"How can I believe you?" Luisito said. "What Cuban agents?"

"Long story," said Agent Stewart, showing the boy and the security guard his badge.

At that moment, several other FBI agents arrived, and Luisito sighed with relief.

Meanwhile, Antonio and Jorge were being escorted into a police car.

"What will happen to them?" Luisito said.

"They will be charged with using a weapon in connection with a crime, conspiracy to kidnapping, and actually trying to kidnap Humberto Gutierrez," said Stewart.

"Will they be sent back?" Luisito asked.

"We won't know until after a lengthy investigation," Agent Stewart said.

"Where is my cousin Tommy?" Luisito said. "He was going to get security."

"He must be in those offices over there being questioned," Stewart said, smiling. "After all, this is a pretty unlikely story for the average person. I will have one of my guys get him."

Then Luisito saw Sonia running in.

"Did I miss anything?" she said.

"Look," Luisito said, pointing at the men in the police car.

When another officer approached to take the blue bag from Luisito, he realized he was still carrying the bag he had taken from Jorge. He looked questioningly at Agent Stewart, who nodded. Luisito gave the bag to the officer.

Agent Stewart, Gutierrez, and the other agent took the blue bag into a security office.

"Please stay back," the officer said to Luisito when he tried to get in and see if the bag held the statue.

"Please, I must see if she arrived," Luisito pleaded.

"Let him come in," Agent Stewart said.

"Where's Tommy?" Sonia asked.

Luisito shrugged his shoulders. "Agent Stewart sent someone to find him," he said.

Inside the room, the officer opened the bag and pulled out the statue of Our Lady of Charity. Her face was porcelain and she had hair like a doll, with a lovely crown adorning her head and a crucifix in her hand. Her dress was a bit torn at the hemline, but she looked beautiful!

"I asked for political asylum at the Panamanian embassy and was waiting to leave the island. I finally got my permission," Gutierrez explained. "I was given the assignment to bring the statue of our Lady to Miami. It was a great honor."

"Did they give you any other instructions?" a young FBI agent asked.

"Yes, I was told that two nuns would approach me at the airport to pick up the image and deliver it to the Cuban priest from *La Ermita*, the shrine of Our Lady of Charity. I was trying to find the nuns," Gutierrez said, "but then those two men came and took the bag, and then he"—Humberto pointed to Luisito— "took the bag from them!"

"Explain to me again, what is so important about this statue?" the young agent asked. "Why would anyone from Cuba want to take it from you?"

"Our Lady of Charity is as much a religious symbol as it is a strong cultural icon. She is the protector of Cuba," Gutierrez explained. "I can only assume that the Cuban government is afraid that this statue coming from Cuba will unite the exile community in this country and bring about changes on the island."

"Interesting," the officer mused.

Agent Stewart signaled to Luisito and Sonia to step out of the office.

"We found Tommy," he said. "He is on his way back from the security offices. I will have a police officer escort you back to your house, and I will personally go with this man to deliver the statue to the priest."

"I want to make sure it gets to Father René de Jesús" Luisito said, worried. He wasn't taking any chances.

"I understand," Agent Stewart said. "I will call you from the priest's office and have him tell you when the statue arrives in his office."

"Thank you," Luisito said. "I really appreciate that."

About a half-hour later, they arrived at Maricusa's house with a police officer escorting them. By now the whole family was worried sick. It had been three hours since they left for the grocery store.

"What happened?" José ran toward the kids and the officer.

"Thank God, you're safe!" Rosie said, limping toward them and hugging them.

The officer asked to come into the house, and they all took a seat to hear him explain. Luisito could see many of the neighbors on the block whispering. He knew that as soon as the policeman left they would have many visitors and that this story would be retold many times.

"They had my permission," Rosie admitted. "I was going to take them myself but then I hurt my foot. I'm sorry, but I had to do my part for our Cuban people here, and I couldn't betray Luisito or Tía Maria Elena's trust."

"There is always more to your grandmother than we can ever imagine!" Miguel said, smiling at Luisito.

✦ ✦ ✦

The family had been invited to a special Mass in honor of the arrival of the statue of Our Lady of Charity in Miami. The statue would be unveiled for all to see. Luisito and his family walked into a massive stadium for the Mass in honor of the feast day of Our Lady of Charity. The soft breeze eased the warm temperature. The bleachers at Miami Stadium were packed. All Luisito could hear were Spanish words being spoken with Cuban accents by those around him. He observed how a television reporter covering the event estimated the crowd at 30,000 people.

The Mass was celebrated in English by Archbishop Coleman Carroll and a group of other priests. In the entrance procession, the statue of Our Lady of Charity was carried on a pedestal by several young men who had come to the United States as part of the Pedro Pan exodus in the early 1960s. The pedestal was adorned with flowers. They carried her all the way to the altar that had been set up in the stadium. The image had been carefully cleaned, her hair combed, and her new white dress sewn with lace trimmings. The crowd cheered and people wept as they gazed on the image, and many waved white handkerchiefs. Many of the children knelt as she passed and greeted her by making the sign of the cross.

At the end of the Mass the crowd went wild, clapping loudly nonstop as Archbishop Carroll blessed them and sent them off with the only two words he knew in Spanish, "*¡Buenas noches!*"

Filled with emotion, Archbishop Carroll began to cry, and so did Luisito as he hugged his mother.

Luisito felt great pride and satisfaction that he had helped to bring the original copy of this statue to the Cuban exiles. When he lived in Cuba, he wasn't able to do much about anything. Here in the United States, he could make a real difference. He was sitting in a row with his parents, Rosie, and their Miami relatives. Luisito fingered the beautiful silver pocket crucifix he had received from Father René Jesus for his help in bringing the statue to safety.

Luisito had never seen so many people crying. So many Cubans in the United States were wishing for Cuba to be free and praying for those they had been forced to leave behind. His was not the only family separated. There were thousands of people who still awaited their parents, spouses, and other relatives who had not received permission to leave. *La Virgen de la Caridad del Cobre* gave them hope.

# 39 TREINTA Y NUEVE

The arrest of the Cuban men who tried to steal the statue of Our Lady of Charity and the possibility that they were indeed spying for the Cuban government was much talked about at Luisito's house, but it only made a paragraph in the international section of most U.S. newspapers.

Luisito was concerned about Abuela and the repercussions that the situation might cause for her back home. The family had requested a call to Cuba and were waiting for the operator to connect them. They could not just pick up the phone and call Cuba because there was no direct line. This was the third time they had tried. The previous times the operator said no one was answering, which caused them even more anxiety.

Although concerned, the family went on with Christmas plans, hoping that they would hear from Abuela soon. José and Miguel came out with some boxes of lights and ornaments to decorate Maricusa and Manuel's front lawn. Many of the neighbors already had lights on their roofs and nativity scenes, plastic snowmen, and reindeer in their yards.

Luisito noticed something he hadn't realized before. Many of the houses on their block had wreaths on the door. These circular arrangements where just like the ones he'd seen at the funerals in Cuba.

"What does this mean, José?" Luisito asked, pointing to the wreath they were about to place on the door. "Did you buy this *corona* at the funeral home?"

"At the funeral home! Oh, no, coronas, or crowns, are used for funerals in Cuba, but in America they're for decoration," José said, laughing. "These are called Christmas wreaths. It's an American tradition."

"Really?" Luisito said, laughing. "If my friends back home only knew about this!"

Miguel asked José to help him untangle the Christmas lights to place around the house. Rosie and Elena were helping Maricusa prepare dinner inside. Although concern for Abuela still weighed heavy on their minds, they wanted to celebrate the birth of Jesus. It was Luisito's first Christmas ever, since the celebration of Christmas was forbidden in Cuba.

Sonia arrived in the kitchen and started preparing the Christmas eggnog. Tommy and Luisito were almost finished decorating the Christmas tree. Maricusa and Manuel called them over to see the beautiful *Nacimiento*. They had all worked a little bit each night on preparing an elaborate nativity set on one side of the living room.

*"Mi niño,"* Maricusa said, hugging Luisito. "My dear boy, don't you worry about your abuela. I know you are thinking about her. We all are, but I learned a long time ago that she is very resourceful, a very clever woman with a lot of faith."

"Thank you," Luisito said, nodding in agreement.

"I'm sure she is all right and wants you to enjoy her favorite holiday!" Maricusa said.

"Why don't you put the star on the tree, Abuelo," Sonia asked while holding her camera.

"Let Miguel do it," Manuel said. "This is his first Christmas in a free land."

Miguel thanked him but said he thought it would be best for Luisito to do it. "It's Luisito's first Christmas celebration ever."

Luisito didn't even have to stand on the stepping stool. As he hung the star everyone applauded and Rosie turned the tree lights on. What a sight! Luisito looked around at his family in the bright glow of the tree. He felt a lump on his throat. He wanted to cry but held it in.

After so many years of living in Cuba with just his parents and grandmother, Luisito now felt so much a part of a large family who cared deeply for him. The Christmas music and the laughter of his family, the lit tree, and the aroma of the food coming from the oven— these were the kind of dreams he had often had in Cuba.

A short but heartfelt prayer came spontaneously: *Thank you, God. Thank you.*

The doors of the house reminded Luisito of a hotel's revolving doors as his family, friends, and neighbors came to visit. They arrived balancing trays of food covered with aluminum foil and wrapped Christmas presents of different shapes.

Two long tables were set in the dining room, with a round one by the living room for the younger crowd. Manuel suggested that Miguel say the prayer before the meal.

"Thank you, God, for bringing us here," said Miguel, his voice choking with emotion. "We are truly blessed. Thank you for a wonderful family that has welcomed and helped us in this new and wonderful country. Please be with Maria Elena in these difficult times. Bless us and this food which we are about to receive. Be with our family and friends in Cuba. May our next Christmas be in a free Cuba!"

"*¡Viva Cuba libre!*" yelled an elderly uncle from across the table.

"*¡Viva!*" yelled the other adults raising their cups.

"They repeat the same thing every year," whispered Sonia to Luisito.

"What do they repeat?" Luisito asked.

"The part about spending the next Christmas in Cuba, and then they yell *viva Cuba libre*," Sonia said. "They've done it for as long as I can remember. Do they ever get tired? I mean, of wishful thinking, year after year."

Luisito just grinned at her. He realized that while he was in Cuba thinking that his family in the United States had forgotten them, they had been praying and hoping to be reunited. Then he remembered Abuela all alone in their apartment. He hoped she knew that they were praying for her.

After dinner, they opened presents. Luisito received some new clothes and a really nice watch from the Galleti family, and a beautiful framed picture of Our Lady of Charity from Maricusa and Manuel. Before he could let it all sink in, it was time for group pictures.

Then everyone drove to Saint Timothy Church in southwest Miami for midnight Mass. The church, while elegant, felt small and cozy. The sweet voices of the schoolchildren made Luisito feel he was surrounded by angels. The music swelled from soft and melodious to loud and joyful. Bright red poinsettias and beautiful porcelain statues of Saint Joseph and the Blessed Mother carrying the infant Jesus adorned the altar.

The smell of pine trees set around the altar permeated the room. Everything was so blissful—bells ringing, the organ playing, and trumpets sounding. Luisito prayed that Abuela would join them soon. He prayed hard. Sometimes he wished he were back in a free Havana. He missed his birthplace—but other times, like tonight, he felt he never wanted to go back. This country was becoming his home and he loved it.

# 40 CUARENTA

On New Year's Eve, back in Maryland, Luisito woke up to shrieks and laughter. Elena was holding a letter from Abuela postmarked early December.

*Dear Luisito, my beautiful daughter Elena, and my wonderful son-in-law Miguel,*

*I hope you are preparing for this wonderful time when we await the birth of el Niño, Jesus! Prepare, prepare! Muchos cariños, all my love, to my sister Maricusa, Rosie, and the whole family. I am fine. Do not worry about me. This is the season of hope and the new year will bring with it many good things.*

*Hugs and kisses, Abuela*

*Exodus 32:1–35*

"There she goes again!" Luisito exclaimed. "This is

the part of the clue that we haven't figured out yet. We need to prepare for something!"

"I wonder what she is talking about?" Elena said.

"Well, whatever it is, she is way smarter than all of us because none of us can decipher it," Tommy added.

"I will call Father René de Jesús and let him know that she is still mentioning it," Luisito said, reaching for the phone.

Everyone paused for a moment, but then they continued taking turns wondering what Abuela meant by the message in the letter.

"Father René de Jesús can't figure it out, either," Luisito said after finishing his phone call. "I spoke to his secretary, Sister Therese, and she said not knowing the code makes her feel very uneasy."

Preparations for New Year's Eve continued. Luisito was separating groups of twelve grapes into tiny bowls for all the family and friends who were gathered at Rosie's house for the celebration. It was a Hispanic tradition that when the clock struck midnight, they would all eat their grapes and make wishes for the new year.

Sherry was invited to the gathering. She was wearing a bright lime-green dress. Luisito wore one of Tommy's dark brown suits.

"You should be so proud of yourself, Lewis," Sherry said. "Your family must be very pleased that you were able to help keep the statue of our Lady safe! Really, how many times does anyone have the opportunity to do something so meaningful? My life is boring compared to yours!"

"Everyone's life is meaningful," Luisito said, smiling. "We all have a purpose that only God knows."

Five minutes before midnight Sonia lowered the music, and everyone gathered around the TV set to see the New Year's countdown from New York's Times Square. Even the lights were lowered so that only the glow of the color TV brightened the dim room.

"Three, two, one . . . Happy New Year! 1980!" Everyone in the room cheered. Luisito gave Sherry a hug.

"I have your Christmas present," he said. "I know it's late, but I wanted you to have this." He took out a small package and handed it to her.

Sherry tore off the wrapping paper and opened the small box. Inside she found a gold chain with a beautiful, delicate medal of Our Lady of Charity.

"It's beautiful!" she whispered. "It will always remind me of the brave Cuban boy I know."

Luisito reached out and gave her a hug. Her hair smelled of lavender. She smiled back at him and they walked over toward Elena and Miguel on the other side of the room. Luisito saw the tears in his mother's eyes and knew that she was sharing in his mixed feelings about this new year. He was sure that great things would happen in 1980, but there was always the uncertainty of tomorrow. Who would have known that last year would involve an escape from Cuba and a move to the United States? What would happen to Abuela in the coming year?

"Everything is going to be all right, Mami," Luisito said. He wasn't sure he believed his own words, but somehow in a strange way he trusted. He hugged his parents.

The chatter continued and the music played. Luisito went to get his bowl of grapes. He had only one wish—that Abuela would be safe.

# 41 CUARENTA Y UNO

**M**ati took Abuela to the Peruvian embassy, where the cook and his kitchen staff found room for her. She requested political asylum at the embassy and hid for days in an office with a sofa bed. One day as she was talking to a woman in the office, they heard a terrible sound. It shook the ground. A bus had intentionally crashed into the iron gates of the embassy. She heard people screaming and running into the Peruvian embassy seeking political asylum; others who were just walking by saw the gates wide open and seized the opportunity to run inside. Children and parents were jumping the other side of the fence to come in. It was just as

Mati had predicted, based on all the comments she had heard about the people's desperation.

Abuela was frightened. She had never seen so many hundreds of desperate people, all running inside with small children and babies. They remained inside the embassy for several weeks. It was a very unpleasant time, because the crowd was hungry, confused, and anxiety-ridden.

"Is there anything to eat?" they would plead.

There was no way to obtain food for so many people. The crowd began to eat the fruit hanging from the trees on the grounds and even the leaves from the bushes.

The Peruvian ambassador, in order to provide assistance, started emptying all the food from the pantry and kitchen. As the weeks wore on, people ate anything they could find, even raw potatoes! It was not ordinary hunger, but one that gnawed deep inside the pit of the stomach. They were weak and they would eat anything to survive.

Mati had decided to remain at the embassy and ask for political asylum as well. She was friends with the cook, who helped her sneak food to the room where Abuela remained hiding. She and Abuela would eat the dry left-over rice, bread, and even potato skins. But Abuela could not bear to see the people suffering from  hunger. She went to the kitchen and asked the cook for chicken bones and onions. She cut up pieces of hard bread and chopped the onions that were left. They put it all in a pot and simmered it to make some soup. She helped fill bowls; then they washed them and filled them again for the rest of the people. The soup wasn't much, but it was warm and had flavor.

Then, surprisingly, the Cuban government gave permission for people from the United States to pick up their relatives on boats. One day, they called Mati to leave in a boat. Mati grabbed Abuela and took her with her. There was so much commotion that no one realized they were leaving. Abuela prayed all along the way. What she feared so much was now her destiny: a boat and the open seas. She prayed as she faced a crowd that was yelling and throwing rocks at her and all the others who were leaving.

Despite everything, she felt calm and peaceful. In the midst of the violence all around her, she knew that God was with her. She clutched her rosary as she made way toward the boat. The first lines of Psalm 27 that Abuela had read so many times came spontaneously to her mind: *The Lord is my light and my salvation; whom should I fear? The Lord is my life's refuge; of whom should I be afraid?*

The man checking names on a clipboard before boarding didn't even notice when Mati pulled Abuela into the boat with her. Abuela mingled with strangers. She didn't see anyone familiar. As the boat embarked, Abuela felt as if she were in some kind of dream—or nightmare.

# 42 CUARENTA Y DOS

After what seemed to Luisito like a very long winter, spring finally came. Everyone in the neighborhood was playing outside, walking and jogging around the neighborhood, and planting anything green, pink, and purple. It was as if the town had come alive with color.

"Oh my!" Luisito heard his mother yell from the living room.

"I can't believe it!" his father echoed.

He heard the commotion grow louder and came running down the stairs to see what was going on. He couldn't make out what his relatives were saying.

"Look at that," Tommy said, glued to the TV set.

"It's amazing!" said Sonia, still in her pajamas.

"What happened?" Luisito asked. A breaking news segment showed people in Miami, some in their cars honking their horns, others running through the streets with signs that read *Cuba Libre! A Free Cuba!*

People of all ages were shown waving the Cuban single-star flag out their car windows. Some people being interviewed in the streets were choked up with emotion.

"This may be the end of communism in Cuba!" an agitated man said. "The Cuban people can't stand it anymore!"

The newscaster began talking about reports of a Cuban bus crashing into the Peruvian embassy. When the bus crashed, toppling the iron gate, hundreds of Cuban people took refuge inside, begging for political asylum. Now boat after boat was arriving in Cuba to pick up refugees and take them to Miami.

There was silence in the room. Everyone was shocked by what they were watching taking place in Cuba and by the reaction in Miami. Tommy and Sonia had wide-open mouths. Miguel was hugging Elena as she bit her nails.

"What does this mean? Will they let them stay in the embassy?" Luisito wanted to know.

"I suppose so," José said. "This is just incredible."

"The desperation of these people . . . it's overwhelming!" Rosie said. "They just dropped what they were doing and ran right in through the gate, without a change of clothes or anything."

"This flotilla may be only the beginning of a massive exodus," the TV reporter announced.

"That's it!" Luisito said, jumping up from his seat. "This is what Abuela meant us to prepare for all along. This is the beginning of something big!"

He rushed to the phone to call Father René de Jesús, who was also watching the television reports and had come to the same conclusion. Father had just called Catholic Charities and asked them to start preparing to help all the refugees that were arriving.

For days, the whole family was glued to the television. The Cuban government, humiliated by the events, said in a statement that anyone who wanted to leave the island could. They saw this as a great opportunity to get rid of all the "problem-causing" citizens: frustrated young people, prisoners, and mental hospital patients. Boats arriving in Cuba from Florida to pick up relatives were forced to take whomever else the government put on their boats. Ninety thousand Cubans arrived in the United States in the month of May alone.

The Cuban government began to discredit the people leaving so they would have a hard time being accepted in the United States. They labeled everyone *"la escoria,"* slang meaning "the scum." Now with all the unrest on the island, there was no way of communicating with Abuela. Although no one said it, everyone feared the worst.

✦ ✦ ✦

Hours after boarding the boat, Abuela started recognizing some familiar faces. In the front of the boat was a family of four. She had seen them before in line at the doctor's office. She saw a female doctor from the hospital, along with some fishermen and several farmers she didn't know by name.

For the next few hours, the weather complied, but the waves were very choppy. She closed her eyes. It was cloudy, so the heat was bearable for now.

"Here, grandmother, take some," the boat's owner said, handing her a water bottle.

They passed out bottles of water for everyone. Abuela took small sips. The water refreshed her dry lips and throat.

The boat was so crowded she wasn't sure if the sweat on her arms was hers or the man's beside her. The spray from the waves gently splashed her face and she felt some relief. Her white-laced blouse was covered with black grease stains. It must have happened when the men helped her onboard. The lace on her collar was torn, and the hemline of her pants was ripped on one side. She held on tightly to her purse. Afraid to lose her rosary, she placed it around her neck.

She held onto the cross with her hand and prayed during the whole trip. It wasn't just a prayer. It was more of a desperate plea to God and his Mother to protect them all from any storms and from capsizing with so many people on board. She fervently prayed for everyone to keep calm and be at peace. Her thoughts drifted from prayer to worries. She thought about her poor family not knowing about her all this time. If the boat capsized and she died, no one would know she was on board. She hadn't told anyone she was going to the embassy, and no one except those on the boat knew she was there. Would she ever get to see her family again? She preferred to focus on how happy their faces would be when they found out about her arrival. That thought kept her strong.

# 43 CUARENTA Y TRES

It was heart-wrenching to have no news from Abuela. It became harder and harder to get any calls through to Cuba now because everyone was trying to call their relatives. Elena finally got a call through to the neighbors. They confirmed that they hadn't seen Abuela and that she hadn't responded to the knocks on her door. Finally, one neighbor pried the door open and found no Abuela and no sign of a struggle. Miguel and Elena knew that when someone disappeared unexpectedly it often meant that the government had kidnapped them.

It was unbearable to think that Abuela may have been tortured and put to death. Luisito and his parents tried finding comfort at church.

It was difficult for Miguel and Elena because they still couldn't communicate well enough in English to speak to the priest. Elena felt empty every time she went to Mass because she couldn't understand English well enough.

One day after Mass, Elena was standing to the side as Rosie and José chatted with the priest. An older priest, Father Carlini, stopped to say hello.

"Where are you from, Elena?" he asked after they had introduced themselves.

"Cuba, Father," she replied.

"Cuba? Ah, there is so much going on there right now. Do you still have family there? Have you heard from them?"

Elena paused. There was so much she wanted to tell the priest, so much to ask his advice about, but she couldn't say it in English. "I'm sorry . . . my English . . ."

"It's okay. I understand," Father Carlini said. He took out a piece of paper and wrote down the name of a priest from another parish who spoke Spanish.

"He can help you," the priest said slowly so she could understand him. "I am sorry I don't speak Spanish, but soon we will have a Spanish priest at our parish. There are a lot of Spanish-speaking people coming, and we want to help them with a Mass in their language."

*"Gracias,"* Elena said happily.

"Miguel, look," Elena said excitedly on the way home. "I have the name and phone number of a priest who speaks Spanish!"

Several times in the next few weeks, Elena and Miguel visited Father José Perez. He was from Honduras, and he spoke English and Spanish. They were able to go to confession in Spanish, and Father Perez counseled them and provided much support for them in this difficult time.

"Never lose hope, never!" he repeated to them.

The weeks passed, and still no word of Abuela. In the midst of their worry, everyone was preparing for Easter. On Holy Saturday evening, they were all getting ready for the Easter Vigil Mass. It was a very important day for Luisito and a group of five other people who had been preparing for months. At this Mass, they would be receiving the sacraments and becoming members of the Church. Luisito had been secretly baptized in Cuba, but he had not received his first Communion or Confirmation. During his preparation, he not only learned about the sacraments and why it was important to receive them, but he also studied the faith and asked many questions. This was only the beginning of his journey in the faith. He felt a strong desire to continue to learn as much as he could. It was in learning about God that Luisito felt closer to him. It made him want to pray and learn more about being a Christian.

Luisito looked at himself in the mirror and thought about the past several months. He had learned so much about God and how different his life was with God in it now. He gelled his blond hair with his fingers and ran a comb through it.

Just then, the doorbell rang. Then it rang again, more urgently. It was probably Maricusa and Manuel, Luisito thought. They had said they were coming to see Luisito receive first Communion and Confirmation. Everyone was still getting dressed, so Luisito ran downstairs and opened the door.

"*Hola*, Maricusa," he said. "I am so glad you made it to my special day!"

Maricusa and Manuel came in and closed the door behind them.

"Everyone, Maricusa and Manuel are here!" Luisito yelled.

Everyone flocked to the door to hug Maricusa and Manuel.

"Mami, you should have let us pick you up at the airport," Rosie said. "Why did you want to take a taxi?"

"My dear, you pick me up all the time. I knew you would be busy today with preparations for Luisito's big day," Maricusa said. Then, looking around, she asked, "Where is your mother, Luisito?"

"Mami, come on! We are waiting for you," Luisito yelled.

Elena came downstairs, straightening her new coral-pink dress. She looked at everyone in amazement.

"What's going on?" she asked. Then she saw Maricusa, her mother's sister, who reminded her so much of her mother. She gave her a big hug.

"We still haven't heard from Mother," Elena whispered to her sadly.

The doorbell rang again and Luisito went to open the door.

He gasped. He stood there, dumbfounded. Was he dreaming? Right in front of his eyes stood Abuela! A much thinner and frailer Abuela, but his dear Abuela all the same!

The silence in the room erupted into shrieks of crying and laughing.

"Abuela! Abuela!" was all Luisito could say as he hugged her tighter and tighter.

Elena and Miguel, teary eyed, embraced her.

"How did this happen?" Elena asked her mother, still embracing her.

"It's a long story," Abuela said, looking up with teary eyes from hugging Luisito.

"Come in, sit down," Rosie said pointing to the sofa.

"You can't imagine," Abuela said. "You remember Mati, our former housekeeper? She took me to the Peruvian embassy a few days before the bus crashed there. The horrible things I saw there ... the people were desperate. It is difficult to speak about."

"Well, tell us, how did you get here?" Miguel wanted to know.

"I was thrown into a boat, all with the help of Mati, who had heard that the Communists were after me. I owe it all to her."

"Where is she now?" Luisito asked.

"She stayed in Miami with a relative. Maricusa is going to help her settle in and find work," Abuela said. "Oh, my Luisito, you look so different, a grown-up man now."

"When did you arrive?" Elena asked.

"Just yesterday, I received a call," Maricusa said. "We picked her up at a hangar filled with thousands of refugees."

"Over one hundred thousand!" Manuel chimed in.

"But Tía, why didn't you call us?" Elena said.

"It was my idea. I wanted to come up here to see you in person," Abuela said. "Besides, I looked like a wreck when I arrived!"

"*Al fin, Abuela.* We are finally together!" Luisito said.

"My dear little one, who is not so little anymore," Abuela said smiling. "You accomplished the mission for me. Maricusa told me all about it. I knew you could do it!"

"Oh, Abuela, that's another story," Luisito said. "I have so many things to tell you."

"Well, we have to be going or else you will not be able to receive the sacraments!" Miguel said.

Abuela listened to Luisito's story about the Cuban spies on the way to church.

"I'm very proud of you, Luisito!" Abuela said. "You were so clever and brave!"

"Just like my grandmother!" Luisito said, and he gave her a big kiss.

They could hear bells ringing from the church tower as they approached the Sacred Heart Church parking lot. The altar was filled with baskets of white calla lilies and other spring flowers. The mood was as joyous inside the building as it was in Luisito's heart. Pews were crowded with parishioners greeting one another. Little girls wore festive spring hats with pastel dresses and matching white purses. The younger boys restlessly turned around in the pews and waved at people coming in. The choir stood tall in the section by the altar, wearing long white and purple robes. Some people were passing out small candles for the entrance procession.

Luisito scanned the space and located his Maryland relatives sitting all together in the front. He saw them whispering to one another as he walked in with his grandmother, probably asking themselves, *Is it really her?* Then Maricusa, who was walking in with them, pointed at Abuela and nodded her head. Luisito had to let go of Abuela's arm as his cousins came rushing down the aisle to hug her. Tears started running down his cheeks. When he had first arrived in this country he had been so happy to have made the journey alive that there was no room for any other emotion. It was different with his grandmother. He had thought she was dead. And now here they were in church, the place that reminded him so much of Abuela, that gave him strength and peace. It was so meaningful that this was the day he was reunited with Abuela. It was like God's present to him.

Someone came to bring Luisito to the church entry way so he could walk in with the group of people receiving the sacraments that night. Luisito kissed Abuela and walked back. He waved at Sherry, who was sitting with her parents.

The pastor of Sacred Heart Church, the Reverend Ed Stack, began the ceremony by lighting the Easter fire. Led by the paschal candle, the procession moved from the entrance into the church. It looked more beautiful than ever. The lights were dimmed and everyone's candles glowed in the dark.

Back in the pew, Abuela took a handkerchief from her purse.

"I would have never imagined seeing all my family in church with me," she whispered to Elena.

"I know, mother," Elena said. "We were in so much fear in Cuba, we just couldn't think straight. Miguel and I are now attending Mass regularly. The sacraments and prayer have truly strengthened us. Rosie and José have also helped us in so many ways."

"*Ay, mi hija,* I'm so glad to hear that," Abuela said. "I have so much to be thankful for. Look at my Luisito walking in with the pastor to receive his first Communion and Confirmation. I never thought I would see this. It's a new beginning for all of us!"

Near the stained-glass window in the back of the church, someone spotted Abuela. How could this be? He focused closer with his lens. It was she, all right. Her face was right on target. The man's trembling finger pressed the button and . . . click, click, click. The sound was muffled by the music and the growing whisper of the people speaking to one another in the pews. The man's camera captured Abuela's smiling face. He took out his white handkerchief and cleaned the sweat from his forehead. Back on the island this would not come as good news, he thought. Abuela and her grandson, together in the United States, could only mean double trouble!

# EPILOGUE

## Fact and Fiction in Mission Libertad

This story is a work of fiction, but the experiences of Luisito and his family are based on real historical events. Their story is full of true anecdotes from other Cubans interviewed who arrived in this country by sea during the 1980s, when the author was a newspaper reporter in South Florida.

+ The statue of our Lady of Charity was commissioned by Monsignor Armando Jiménez Rebollar in 1947 in Cuba. It is a copy of the original found floating at sea.

The statue was smuggled out of Cuba by the Archdiocese of Havana through the Italian embassy, which then passed it to Panama's embassy in Cuba. It finally arrived in the United States not in 1979, when the story takes place, but in 1961.

* The man who actually brought the statue was not named Humberto Gutierrez but Luis Gutiérrez Areces.

* The Mass by Bishop Coleman Carroll took place as mentioned in the book, but not in 1979. The Mass was celebrated in Miami Stadium on September 8, 1961.

* In reality, there were no spies—that we know of— trying to capture the statue.

* There have been several notorious cases confirmed and reported in U.S. newspapers of Cuban spies in the United States who have been arrested and tried. Some fled to Cuba. Those events are what inspired the spy story in this book.

* It is true that this statue of our Blessed Mother is now displayed in *La Ermita de la Caridad,* the shrine of Our Lady of Charity, in Miami, Florida, for anyone who wishes to visit.

* In the time this story takes place, Cuban children and their families arrived in Florida by homemade rafts

and were allowed to stay in this country if they feared persecution in the island. This was allowed under the 1966 Cuban Adjustment Act, but during the administration of President Bill Clinton the act was re-interpreted to mean only the Cuban rafters who reached dry U.S. soil could stay. This new policy is still enforced and is known informally as the wet foot/dry foot policy. Cubans found at sea are now sent back to Cuba or to a third country, while those Cubans who reach U.S. soil are allowed to remain in the United States.

+ In some cases, if a person found at sea has a valid case for political asylum, they may be sent to Guantanamo base in Cuba for further review.

+ It is true that thousands of Cubans fleeing communism by rafts have perished in the ocean during the dangerous journey. There have been cases of others drowning at sea trying to swim away from the U.S. Coast Guard, which would send them back to Cuba.

+ Most Cubans are forbidden to leave the island, even to travel on vacation, unless the Cuban government approves. Their food is rationed, everything is owned by the government, and they do not have some basic human rights such as freedom to express their opinions.

+ Just like Abuela in the story, Cubans entered the Peruvian embassy in 1980. In just twenty-four hours, thousands of Cubans—men, women, and children—packed the embassy, trying to flee Cuba. This prompted the Mariel Boatlift, in which more than 125,000 Cubans, from April to October 1980, sailed from Cuba's Mariel Harbor to the straits of Florida.

+ Millions of Cubans have arrived to the United States during the years in various exoduses: the Camarioca Boatlift, Freedom Flights, Pedro Pan, the Mariel Boatlift, and in rafts by sea.

**Who:** The Daughters of St. Paul

**What:** Pauline Teen—linking your life to Jesus Christ and his Church

**When:** 24/7

**Where:** All over the world and on www.pauline.org

**Why:** Because our life-long passion is to witness to God's amazing love for all people!

**How:** Inspiring lives of holiness through: Apps, digital media, concerts, websites, social media, videos, blogs, books, music albums, radio, media literacy, DVDs, ebooks, store, conferences, bookfairs, parish exhibits, personal contact, illustration, vocation talks, ph-- writing, editin--

BOOKS & MEDIA

The Daughters of St. Paul operate book and media centers at the following addresses. Visit, call or write the one nearest you today, or find us on the World Wide Web, www.pauline.org

CALIFORNIA

| | |
|---|---|
| 3908 Sepulveda Blvd, Culver City, CA 90230 | 310-397-8676 |
| 935 Brewster Avenue, Redwood City, CA 94063 | 650-369-4230 |
| 5945 Balboa Avenue, San Diego, CA 92111 | 858-565-9181 |

FLORIDA

| | |
|---|---|
| 145 S.W. 107th Avenue, Miami, FL 33174 | 305-559-6715 |

HAWAII

| | |
|---|---|
| 1143 Bishop Street, Honolulu, HI 96813 | 808-521-2731 |
| Neighbor Islands call: | 866-521-2731 |

ILLINOIS

| | |
|---|---|
| 172 North Michigan Avenue, Chicago, IL 60601 | 312-346-4228 |

LOUISIANA

| | |
|---|---|
| 4403 Veterans Memorial Blvd, Metairie, LA 70006 | 504-887-7631 |

MASSACHUSETTS

| | |
|---|---|
| 885 Providence Hwy, Dedham, MA 02026 | 781-326-5385 |

MISSOURI

| | |
|---|---|
| 9804 Watson Road, St. Louis, MO 63126 | 314-965-3512 |

NEW YORK

| | |
|---|---|
| 64 West 38th Street, New York, NY 10018 | 212-754-1110 |

PENNSYLVANIA

| | |
|---|---|
| Philadelphia—relocating | 215-676-9494 |

SOUTH CAROLINA

| | |
|---|---|
| 243 King Street, Charleston, SC 29401 | 843-577-0175 |

VIRGINIA

| | |
|---|---|
| 1025 King Street, Alexandria, VA 22314 | 703-549-3806 |

CANADA

| | |
|---|---|
| 3022 Dufferin Street, Toronto, ON M6B 3T5 | 416-781-9131 |